ELEANORA E. TATE

Don't Split the Pole

Tales of Down-Home Folk Wisdom

AN AUTHORS GUILD BACKINPRINT.COM EDITION

iUniverse LLC
Bloomington

This book is dedicated to Blackie the Tennessee Farm Dog,
Rex the Missouri Wolf, Malik the noble Brittany Spaniel, Jobie the Iowa Dog,
Jihad the Siamese Cat, Patches of South Carolina,
our Very Most Beloved Cat Rahima, and all the other animals domestic and free,
living and departed, who have done so much to enrich our lives.

Special thanks to Ted Carskadon and Virginia Oliver of Canton, Missouri; and
North Carolina Aquariums at Pine Knoll Shores, Fort Fisher, and Manteo,
North Carolina.
—E.T.

DON'T SPLIT THE POLE
Tales of Down-Home Folk Wisdom

AN AUTHORS GUILD BACKINPRINT.COM EDITION

iUniverse books may be ordered through booksellers or by contacting:

iUniverse LLC
1663 Liberty Drive
Bloomington, IN 47403
www.iuniverse.com
1-800-Authors (1-800-288-4677)

Originally published by Delacorte Press

Because of the dynamic nature of the Internet, any web addresses or links contained in
this book may have changed since publication and may no longer be valid. The views
expressed in this work are solely those of the author and do not necessarily reflect the
views of the publisher, and the publisher hereby disclaims any responsibility for them.

Any people depicted in stock imagery provided by Thinkstock are models,
and such images are being used for illustrative purposes only.
Certain stock imagery © Thinkstock.

ISBN: 978-1-4917-3267-0 (sc)

Printed in the United States of America.

iUniverse rev. date: 05/13/2014

Contents

You Can't Teach an Old Dog New Tricks

Maggie braced all four short fat legs against the sand-sprinkled carpet and pulled against the rope that Joshua had tied to her collar. "I won't do it and I won't go," she growled. "Drag me, hang me, but I ain't going out."

"C'mon, Maggie! Okay, then I'll carry you," Joshua said. He picked her up in his skinny arms and started for the back door.

"And keep her outside till we're completely unpacked," Joshua's mother, Heather, said. "Bad girl, Maggie, bad girl!"

Bad girl? She'd only been looking for her bed so she could take her after-breakfast nap. She was an older dog, and older dogs took lots of naps. Heather knew that. Heather was an older woman, and she took lots of naps, too, now that she'd lost her job at school. If Heather had put Maggie's bed in its usual place, none of this would have been happening. But everything was a mess because they'd moved again.

Maggie, on her own, had finally located her bed, squashed beneath a ton of boxes in their new dining room. When she'd pulled on her bed, stuff inside the boxes made crash and crack sounds as they hit the floor. Heather had gone bananas. They should have all stayed back home in the mountains of North Carolina instead of moving down here to the coast, to Morehead City.

Maggie sneezed and Joshua put her back down on the carpet. The salty air blowing in through the windows made Maggie's nose sting, made her eyes water, and made her eardrums stuffy. The joints in her front legs ached. Was her rheumatism kicking up in this humid air? Where were her water bowl, her after-breakfast snack and medicine, her cabin, her pine trees, her mountains, and her fresh air? So many changes!

"It's all right, girl," said Joshua. "It wasn't your fault. You just want to go back home. Join the crowd." He rubbed Maggie's fat gray basset hound muzzle against his cheek. "Mom, I bet Maggie misses our house in Asheville as much as I do."

"Yes, talk some sense into your momma," Maggie tried to tell him by licking his ears. They were almost as big as hers. One of his front teeth actually was. It was still a baby tooth, but it was so big that Joshua couldn't wait until it fell out and his permanent front tooth grew in. He was praying that it would be regular size—small—like his other ones.

"I bet that's why she keeps getting into things. Mom, maybe you're not supposed to keep moving old dogs from one town to another. Maybe she's too old to learn anything new anymore. I mean, she's sixty-three in dog years, right?"

"Right, but I miss our old house, too. You don't see me knocking over boxes and breaking things." His mother lifted pieces of broken dish out of a box. "Josh, you were so eager to move when Dad first told us about his job transfer down here to Morehead City. And now I can barely get you out of the house. What's made you change your mind?"

"Nothing. But what if the kids call me Bony or Dumbo again?"

"Call them names back. That worked when we lived in California, didn't it? Or just ignore it. At least this time you'll have the rest of June and all of July to make friends before school starts." With her foot, Joshua's mom scraped together a small mound of sand on the carpet. "Honestly, honey, I'm tired of moving, too. This is the fourth time. In two or three years, when Daddy is done here, maybe we can move back to Asheville. Or even back to Georgia to that beach house on Tybee Island. That was nice. You were just a baby then."

"I don't wanna wait two or three years," Joshua mumbled. He picked Maggie back up, pushed the back door open, and let it slam closed. "I wanna go back to Beaver Tail Road, Asheville, North Carolina, right now!"

"Work on her," Maggie grunted, and nudged his arm. "Negotiate a settlement."

Joshua tied Maggie to a tree in the sandy backyard. "Geez, you're heavy," he said. "You need to go on a better diet." Pushing back his blond hair, he squatted beside her and rubbed her big nose. "Mom says I'll get used to this place and meet some nice kids, but I bet I won't. They're gonna laugh at me."

Maggie rolled on her back, paws in the air, so that Joshua could scratch her fat belly. That usually made them both feel better. When he didn't scratch, she raised her head and let her right ear dangle in the sand. She gave him her droopy "poor thing" look. Joshua was supposed to ask, "What's the matter, poor thing?" and then take her on a walk.

Instead Joshua said, "Stay here. The system's crashed, Maggie. That means we're in the pits, with the dragons of gloom. I'm gonna try to set up my computer again. Maybe somebody's e-mailed me. I wish Dad was here to help me. He won't be home till late tonight. I'll be back in a minute, girl," he said, and went back inside.

When he didn't return, Maggie barked loudly to remind him, until she noticed a man sitting on his back porch next door. The man was frowning at her. She turned her attention to him.

"Excuse me," she barked, wagging her tail, "would you tell Joshua that he—"

"Oh no, not another barker," the man said, and stood up. "Be quiet!" He shook his finger at Maggie.

Maggie closed her mouth. She stopped wagging her tail. She sniffed the ground. Sand was everywhere. Sand meant—oh no!—not cats, too! When she was a puppy somewhere else with sand, she'd been chased by vicious cats all the time.

Maggie sniffed around the tree Joshua had tied her to, and smelled the scent of a big hairy dog with lots of slobber. She stiffened. Werewolves? Had to be the dragons of gloom for sure. Maggie sent out several warning-signal barks to Joshua. That set off the neighbor's finger again.

Maggie sniffed at the rope. So uncool, to be tied to a tree with a piece of measly clothesline. She walked round and round the tree until she had wrapped the line so tightly to it that she could just barely breathe in comfort. That ought to do it. Joshua had to come out now. His poor thing was tangled up! When he still didn't come, she howled until she was breathless, her throat was dry, and the man next door was howling and fussing, too.

When she heard another strange noise, she paused. Now what in the Holy Dog Hereafter . . . ? Showing her teeth and growling nervously, Maggie glanced around, then up. Four orange furry legs hung from a branch above her head, and two large yellow-green eyes glared at her.

"Well, well, look what waddled in from the fat-dog farm," the orange cat, who was pretty fat himself, said.

"Shoo, you recycled pile of fuzz," Maggie said, "or I'll pull your tail out through your ears!"

"Oh my, I'm sooo scared! What big teeth you have, and what a big nose! And look at those ears! I'm not one to make fun of anybody, but talk about nothin' but a hound dog! Hey, mutt, how'd you like to get a nice back rub with these?" The cat unsheathed his long, pointy claws and flicked his front paws at her. Then he stood up, arched his back like a Halloween feline, puffed out his tail, and crouched like he was about to spring. "Beat it!" the cat hissed. "This is *my* tree, *my* yard. Scram!"

The sound of wings made the cat pause. A large black, white, and gray bird made a one-footed landing a few feet from Maggie. "Hi there, kiddo. You visiting Oscar?"

Maggie stepped back from the bird, growling and snapping. She was being attacked from all sides now! "Stay back, bird, or I'll snatch every feather off your head!" she said.

The bird, though, was calmly looking up into the tree.

"Don't mind McGuire," the bird told Maggie. "He's all spit and hair balls. Watch." The bird flew up and, squawking, beat his wings in the cat's face. Spitting, McGuire retreated to another branch, crossed stiff-legged onto the roof of Joshua's house, and disappeared around the chimney.

"See what I mean?" the bird said when he returned. "He lives next door at Mr. Killjoy's place. I'm One-Foot. A shark, the dirty devil, bit off my right leg when I was riding the waves during Hurricane Bertha. I was on my way to the state park just now when I heard you howling. I thought Oscar, my Saint Bernard friend, was having another party down here. He sure loved a good time. I guess he's moved on. McGuire hated him. I was gonna take Oscar to lunch, but you're here now, so . . . can I take you to lunch, Miss, er, ah—"

"Oh, excuse me, Mr. One-Foot," Maggie said. This bird sure was talkative! "Please forgive my lack of manners. I'm Maggie, from Asheville." When One-Foot continued to stare at her with his friendly, shiny black eyes, she added, "And thank you for coming by just now. Why, every second I've been here has been just complete chaos. Moving in yesterday was so disorganized."

One-Foot listened carefully while Maggie told him her problems. "Things change, kiddo," he said. "You gotta learn to float with the tide. Living by the ocean's a pretty good shake, though, if you ask me. Weather's great. Food's everywhere. You'll like it. 'Scuse me."

Keeping an eye out for McGuire, Maggie watched One-Foot soar over Killjoy's house, then return and hover in the air near her. "I was checking for tourist buses at the park," he explained. "Folks come and feed us seagulls. We got good eyesight, kiddo. We can see a crow carrying a piece of coal at midnight. That's a bird joke, get it? Are you retired? A lot of retirees move here. Oscar did. I did. I came down from Virginia after working on a fishing trawler."

Maggie hesitated. Truth was, she hadn't worked since the vet put her on sedatives for hyperactivity a long time ago. "I'm, uh, a semiretired security guard. Max—that's Joshua's father—is an accounts troubleshooter with a major corporation, and Joshua's mother, Heather, is a substitute teacher. Joshua's our boy. He's got the most gorgeous ears, and the biggest front tooth on a human that I've ever seen." Maggie sneezed. "But this humidity's rotting off my nose and swelling my legs up into balloons, Joshua's depressed, Heather's gone bananas—so you can understand why I got to get us back to the mountains."

"You'd better part company with that string around your neck first. It's holding you back, if you know what I mean."

Maggie nosed the clothesline. "Yes, but Joshua said stay till he got back. I raised Joshua from a baby," she said proudly, "and taught him all he knows."

"I hope you didn't teach him to tie you to a tree, did ya?" One-Foot chuckled. "Just teasing. C'mon and have lunch. Then you can come back, take a nap, settle in, whatever. The mountains are a million miles away, you know. You might as well forget about walking, and I sure can't fly you on my back. You look like you still got a lotta spring in you, but you keep talking about your rheumatiz and your sinuses and your medicine—whew! I bet you can't even get out the yard without taking a rest."

"Very funny." Grabbing the clothesline with her teeth, Maggie jerked once and *pop!* She was free. She sniffed around the yard, snorting at Oscar's and McGuire's scents and carefully replacing each one with her own.

One-Foot circled overhead. "First bus pulled in, Maggie! Gotta go, girl!" When she still hesitated, he added, "Let's have lunch. Then I can show you where the highway to Asheville is."

"Well . . . all right." Maggie took a deep sniff, sneezed again, and followed One-Foot out of the yard. After she had lunch with One-Foot, she would get Joshua and take that road to Asheville. Then they'd be back *home*. And return to a normal life.

Maggie waddled around the hedges and practically

bumped into Mr. Killjoy, who was watering his rose-
bushes. "Don't you poop in my yard!" he yelled. He
pointed the hose at her. As she rushed around him, she
tripped over the hose and jerked it out of his hands. Like
an attacking green cobra, the hose spit water in Mr.
Killjoy's face. It sent a shower of water against Maggie's
departing white-and-brown rump as she hurried as
quickly as she could after One-Foot. She hadn't moved
that fast since she and Joshua were chased by a skunk
back home.

But that was in her younger years, before the vet said
she was hyperactive and should be slowed down. When
she was still slender. She had always loved to run. And
jump. Panting, Maggie sat down to rest.

"You look like a caterpillar when you run," One-Foot
yelled, "but cute. Let's zip over to the dock at the canal.
There's tasty squid and shrimp over there if you like
seafood. French fries if you like fast food."

"I love everything," Maggie said, "but I'm on a low-
cholesterol diet."

She followed One-Foot along a dirt road that led to
some water. One-Foot flew toward a row of boats tied up
at a wooden dock in a wide canal leading to the bay. He
landed on the railing of a large boat, then hopped down
inside. Maggie followed him to the end of the dock. She
looked down. One-Foot was gobbling pink clumps of

something from a bucket on the floor at the front of the boat.

When she cleared her throat hungrily, One-Foot hopped up onto a bench on the boat's deck and pecked at a sack until its contents spilled out. "All-beef patties, cheese, pickles, onions, catsup, sesame seed buns—and still warm! Jump in!"

Maggie licked her lips. She edged closer to the water as the seagull continued eating. "Jumping isn't the easiest thing for basset hounds to do," she said to him. "We're rather long-waisted."

Have mercy, she hadn't jumped in ages. But Maggie, she asked herself, how will you ever get Joshua back to the mountains if you can't even jump into a boat? And she did need food to keep up her strength.

Well, all for the boy, she thought. She flung herself toward the boat. She landed with a thump on the bench and almost ended up on top of One-Foot.

"Bravo, kiddo! You oughta try out for the Olympics. You *do* still got some spring in ya," said One-Foot.

"Of course I do," Maggie answered. She was pleased and nervous at the same time. She tore at the paper wrappings around the cheeseburgers.

"And jumping's a lot quicker than taking the steps down there at the other end," One-Foot went on.

"What steps?" Only then Maggie noticed the steps leading down into the boat from the boardwalk. "Oh, you're sly," she said. "But thanks anyway." She licked One-Foot on his right wing.

"Aw, kiddo, I didn't do nothing. We old-timers—me and you—gotta keep busy, you know, so we don't get in a rut, not stay so set in our ways. Here." He dropped a beakful of his own meal onto a catsup-covered pickle. "Take a chance and have a real delicacy, fit for a queen. It's good for your diet, too."

"Don't mind if I do." She slurped it down. It tasted like gooey rubber bands in tomato paste. At his insistence she had some more, then ate the other cheeseburger. Maggie looked at One-Foot's single leg. "One-Foot, what's a shark?"

"They're big ugly bullies with a million sharp teeth who swim around attacking innocent birds like me! Garbage Guts is what I call 'em. They'll eat anything."

"Do they eat dogs, too?"

"Sure. Dogs, tin cans, boats, people, anything. Forget 'em. I've put it behind me." One-Foot hopped to the bench seat, knocked over an aluminum can with his wing, and pecked at the liquid that spilled out. "Here. Have a little drink. It's good for your heart. And have some more of this squid. It's so fresh it's almost alive."

Maggie lapped at the liquid and belched. She eyed the slimy purple strings of flesh hanging from One-Foot's

beak. "Raw squid? Er, I've had enough, thank you. I—
What's the matter?"

One-Foot had swung into the air, squawking. "Hide,
hide, quick, quick!"

A man walked toward the boat. Heart pounding, tail
trembling, Maggie scrambled to the back of the boat and
hid behind some buckets. Would the man toss her overboard for eating his food? Would he have her thrown into
the dog pound?

The next thing Maggie knew, the boat was moving
away from the dock. She was terrified and almost barked.
As if he'd read her mind, One-Foot landed on a bucket
beside her. "It's okay, kiddo, we're going deep-sea fishing
with Jorge! Hope you don't get seasick easy. Jorge might
go out to sea for three or four or fifty some miles and be
out all day and all night on this baby, chasing a blue
marlin or a sailfish."

"Oh, great," Maggie groaned. "Now I've been kid-
napped, I'm gonna get eaten up by a Garbage Gut, and
I'll never see my people again. This is so disorganized."

"You were gonna leave 'em for the mountains anyway,
remember?" One-Foot hovered in the air and waggled his
foot at her. "How many other dogs do you know that get
to go deep-sea fishing on a fancy boat like this Grady
White, for cryin' out loud? Organized, schmorganized—
live a little! Don't be such an old fogey. I know Jorge.

He's good people. Now listen, when I give you the word, come out, introduce yourself, have some fun. Right now stay put and keep quiet till I come back, okay? 'Scuse me."

The boat sped out of the canal, under a high-rise bridge, and then into the bay, headed for the sea. The roar of the engine and the slap of the waves hitting the boat replaced the sounds of land. Maggie remained hidden behind the buckets in the hot sun. Out to sea!

Ocean spray gathered in puddles near her back feet. She licked it up, but it only made her thirstier. Maggie and the big boat swayed and bobbed up and down, to the left, to the right, over, and over, and over.

The sun beat down and the minutes passed. Maggie drank more water. Some guard dog she was. Joshua could be in trouble. He was so bony that some nasty dog might be dragging him off and burying him this very minute. Even Heather could be in trouble. But where was Maggie? On a boat headed for the edge of the earth, where she would be swallowed alive by a Garbage Gut.

Maggie laid her muzzle on her paws and moaned to herself. If she could only get back to her boy and her people. Why, she'd tie her own self to a tree. She'd even put up with McGuire, the nasty cat, and sand, and never complain about going *back home* to the mountains again. She'd even lose weight and get lively.

Maybe One-Foot was right. Maybe she *was* in a rut. She *was* an old fogey. But she knew now what she had to do. She would march right up to that Jorge and tell him to return home to Joshua. Joshua needed her. Duty called!

When Maggie got to her feet, it was like when Joshua would pick her up, spin them around in circles, and set her back down. She'd stagger around dizzily for a few minutes, and that was fun, and then he'd do it again. But here, on this boat, on the sickening sea, everything kept whirling around. The boat, the buckets, the sky, her tail, everything was wobbling. Or was it just her eyes and her stomach?

The salty water, the pickles, the catsup, the greasy fried cow meat, the bubbly drink, and the smell and taste of raw purple squid churned and gurgled in her stomach. Which erupted like a volcano. Everything inside came up again and again and again until Maggie's eyes crossed, her nose dripped, and her tail kinked. When she got a chance to open her eyes and breathe, she saw and smelled the mess she'd made. That set her off again.

Slipping in the slimy, fishy, greasy lumps, Maggie forgot One-Foot's advice. She closed her eyes and let loose with a roll of anguished howls. Immediately footsteps thumped to the buckets and stopped next to her paws.

Maggie swallowed. Silence.

Finally she opened one mournful, seasick eye. A man—Jorge—towered above her. She was done for. This Jorge would throw her overboard to be eaten by a Garbage Gut. Good-bye, dear Joshua, good-bye. The system's crashed forever. Maggie belched.

"And who are you?" said Jorge. "Yuck, what a mess. Pee-Yew! So this's where my lunch and my beer went."

Maggie wagged her tail once, weakly. "Aw, poor thing," said Jorge. Holding his nose with his fingers, he knelt down beside her. "You don't look like you're a biter. Looks like you get seasick the way my boy, Eddie, does." He fingered her ID tag. "Maggie, huh? Okay, Maggie, let's clean you up. And get you sober, too."

Sometime later Maggie woke up on a beach towel in the shade at the front of the boat. Jorge stood at the steering wheel in a tiny room above her. Still woozy, she sniffed at a nearby bowl, noticed it was full of fresh—not salty—water, and gratefully lapped it down. Had she died and gone to the Holy Dog Hereafter?

"How ya feel now, kiddo?" said One-Foot, perched on the railing. "Half an hour ago you looked like something not even McGuire would drag in. Jorge gave you an antiseasick pill, but don't look at the ocean or you'll get sick again. Sorry about leaving you for so long. I was talking to the buoys and gulls." One-Foot paused. "That's another bird joke."

Jorge cut the engine and picked up a long fishing rod. "Maggie, I see you're back with the living. I called that telephone number on your tag, and I called the dock office. Don't worry, old girl, we'll get you home. In fact, I'm sticking close to shore with you on board. Don't want you to upchuck again. Maybe you'll be good luck. I'm gonna need it, 'cause my fish-finder screen's gone blank. I'll get Eddie to look at it. He's the computer whiz."

Maggie whimpered a little. "Does this mean we're going home now?" she asked One-Foot.

One-Foot fluttered above Jorge's head. "Oh no, we're going fishing for Spanish mackerel. They're some good eating. Hey, Jorge, how about tossing some squid to a hungry bird?"

At the mention of squid, Maggie's stomach quivered. "Please don't ever use that word around me again," she howled.

"Cut out that noise, Maggie," said Jorge. "I'm trying to concentrate." He cast a red-and-white, bullet-shaped artificial bait with two treble hooks dangling off it into the water. He began to reel it back with quick jerks. Suddenly the rod bent nearly double. Pumping hard, he reeled in a large Spanish mackerel. "Whoa!" He unhooked the fish and dropped it into his cooler. "Maggie, you brought me luck! Howl all you want."

Maggie perked up her ears. That was it! "One-Foot, can you see fish?"

"Of course I can!" the bird replied.

"Great!" said Maggie. "Then when you see another one, tell me, please? I'll howl, Jorge will throw, and maybe he'll catch it. The more he catches, the quicker I'll get home! So if you say when and where, I'll howl."

"Sounds like fun." One-Foot flew high in the air, circled, and then sailed low over the water. "A whole school, to the left!" he squawked.

Maggie nudged Jorge's left ankle with her nose, then howled.

"Here, what'd you poke me for? Oh, I see!" Jorge cast to the left where the water foamed white. Again the rod bent double, and Jorge hauled in another large Spanish mackerel.

"That was a coincidence," Jorge said as he dropped the fish into his cooler. "You howling and me catching another fish. Wasn't it?"

"You're a genius," One-Foot told Maggie. He swooped low again. "Fish to the right!"

For the next several minutes howls, squawks, and shouts split the air as Jorge plugged and caught one Spanish mackerel after another. When the school of fish moved on, Jorge flopped down in his chair. He wiped his sweaty face and brown beard on his T-shirt.

"Nobody's gonna believe me, Maggie. A fish-finding basset hound? So where'd you learn that? Man, that's one noisy seagull. Here!" Jorge threw a handful of squid in the air, and One-Foot expertly caught several pieces before they hit the water. Maggie looked away and held her breath.

"What a team we are, kiddo!" One-Foot said. "This is great. We could knock 'em dead at the piers. Let's go tomorrow, same time, all right?"

"Sure, as long as a pier's not a boat. And I'll bring Joshua." Maggie hadn't howled this much with human approval since New Year's Eve. She felt fine again, at last. "What a day, One-Foot. Can we go home now?"

"Which home do you mean, Maggie?" One-Foot asked.

"My new one."

Jorge started the engine, turning dials and punching buttons at the control panel back in the little room above her. "Good news, girl. That telephone number on your collar is your Asheville vet. He's called your home here in Morehead. Your boy'll be waiting for you at the docks."

When Jorge's boat entered the canal, Maggie saw the tiny figures of Joshua and Heather grow larger and larger on the dock. She barked and danced from one foot to another. As soon as Jorge had steered the boat parallel to the boardwalk, Maggie scrambled up the steps and ran to where Joshua kneeled with his arms outstretched. She threw herself against his small chest and licked his face and big ears.

"Oh, Maggie, we've been looking for you all day," said Joshua. "Yuck! You smell like rotten fish. You okay?" He looked up at Jorge and put one hand in front of his mouth as he talked. "Thanks, mister."

"Maggie's one in a million," Jorge said, and introduced himself. "I never caught so many Spanish mackerel in such a short time in my life. Where'd she learn how to do that?"

"I have no idea," said Heather. "I guess an old dog can teach *herself* new tricks."

"Joshua, my son Eddie's about your age," said Jorge. "If I can drag him away from his computer, maybe I'll take you both fishing."

"He likes computers? Cool! Mom, maybe Eddie can come help me get my computer working." Joshua hid his tooth with his forearm as he talked.

"I think he'd like that," said Jorge, and gave Joshua his telephone number. "I think he'd like to show you his big front tooth, too."

On the walk back home, Maggie trotted ahead of Joshua and Heather. She was practicing jumping along the way, when she remembered that she hadn't taken any medicine that day. She jumped over a twig on the sidewalk. Maybe she didn't need so much medicine. "Oh, I am so glad to be off that boat!" she barked to One-Foot. "Back with Joshua again! Where's McGuire? Hold me back, One-Foot, or I'll chew him up!" She bounded after a palmetto bug skittering across the grass.

"Geez, Maggie, I've never seen you so energetic," said Joshua. "Mom, what's got into her?"

"I don't know," his mother said, "but whatever it is, I want some, too."

A Hard Head Makes a Soft Behind

Russell James slapped at a mosquito and checked his watch again. His uncle, Bron Kitis, had been squatting in water up to his armpits in the middle of Troublesome Creek since five o'clock, trying to catch a catfish with his hands. Now it was almost sunset. He hadn't caught one yet.

"Uncle Bron, you might as well quit," Russell said from where he stood in the shallow water. "Bet I coulda caught a twenty-five-pounder two hours ago. Come on and do something. It's gonna get dark out here pretty soon."

"I been catching more cats with this one finger"— Uncle Bron held up his wet right hand and wiggled his stub of remaining thumb—"longer than your momma, your daddy, and you put together. I know what I'm doing. You haven't even caught one the way I do, and I'm not about to let you try till you turn ten. So pipe down."

"I could catch one if you'd let me," Russell replied. He flipped his brown hair back from his eyes. "You haven't even caught a cooter today. You haven't even caught a minnow."

"And don't want to." Uncle Bron went back to working his hands in and out of the underwater caves that the old cypress tree roots had made. He came up empty-handed again. "Don't get me started, Russell James. I don't want to make you get to bawling if I got to tease you. You know you can't take teasing like I can. Teasing don't bother me."

Russell knew it didn't, which was why he liked to do it. But Russell knew not to tease his uncle too much when it came to hand fishing. Uncle Bron hated to have to come home empty-handed from fishing. Bron Kitis was the Hand Fish King of Nutbrush County, Missouri. He had been written up in the *Kansas City Star* and *USA Today* newspapers and the *Missouri Conservationist*. The newspaper over in Canton had run a picture of Uncle Bron holding up a fifty-five-pound flathead he'd caught with his hands. Uncle Bron used his secret McCutcheon Clutch to catch them. But the McCutcheon Clutch hadn't brought in anything so far this evening. Everybody knew that next to nighttime—when the really, really monster catfish came out—evening was the best time to catch fish.

Another thing Russell knew not to ever, ever, *ever* tease his uncle about was his name. Russell's great-aunt had gotten sick with a bad cold just before Uncle Bron was born. Russell's great-uncle had said that Bron was "sneezed" into the world, and named him Bron Kitis in memory of the occasion. But Uncle Bron Kitis said neither his name nor the story was funny. Anybody caught laughing at his name might as well get ready to fight.

"Uncle Bron, let me try. I know how. I've watched you and Daddy enough times. I don't need to wait six more months." Russell spread his left thumb and fingers into a fierce-looking claw. "I bet I can snatch up a twenty-pound cat."

"Yeah, and I bet something'd snatch you up and pull you under with it just as easy," Uncle Bron said. "A twenty-pound cat fights like it weighs two hundred. You can barely lift up your own feet, let alone twenty pounds. You fumble around under the water not knowing what you're doing and you're liable to grab up a ten-foot-long copperhead."

Uncle Bron stopped and looked around. Russell did, too. Poisonous snakes like copperheads, water moccasins, and rattlers liked to hang out around Troublesome Creek. Russell thought he'd seen a copperhead earlier around the concrete pilings where the old bridge had toppled into the creek.

"You gotta grow some more before you start hand

fishing," Uncle Bron went on. "So put down 'get bigger' for number eleven on your Turn Ten List."

Russell laughed. "I only got three things on my Turn Ten List. Number one is by the time I turn ten Dad'll be back home from Kuwait. Number two is Mom'll buy me that motorized trail bike, and number three is I'll snatch up a fifty-pound catfish in my McCutcheon Clutch. I might as well do number three right now. Come on, I'm getting bored. I'm tired of always waiting."

"Pipe down so I can concentrate. Your yapping's scaring off my fish."

Russell frowned. He waded upstream from his uncle. He pulled a slingshot and a chunk of gravel out of his camouflage pants pocket and shot the rock toward a weeping willow tree. The gravel thunked against the tree, sent a blue jay squawking—and plunked down on Uncle Bron's head.

Russell sucked in his breath. "Sorry, Uncle Bron. I was aiming at the tree. I about knocked all the tail feathers off that blue jay."

"And about knocked the last hair off my head," said Uncle Bron, who was almost bald. "Put that thing up before you hurt somebody. I don't eat blue jays. I eat chicken and catfish."

"Looks like we're gonna have to settle for chicken,

then. Was this what Momma meant when she said you were slowing down?"

"Said what?" Uncle Bron raised up, frowning. "Hunh. Don't you worry about who's slowing down," he said with a little snap to his voice. "Just you watch and learn. And be quiet."

"I could catch a blue channel cat bigger than the one that swam off with your thumb," Russell went on. Uncle Bron stayed silent. Russell added, "Momma said it was a snapping turtle that bit it off anyway, not a catfish."

Uncle Bron's face turned red. "My sister's all talk and you're all tease. Don't get too smart for your britches now. A smart mouth makes a soft behind. A hard head makes a soft one, too."

Slapping at a deerfly, Uncle Bron moved to a more shallow spot near a sycamore tree and bent over again. Russell aimed at a squirrel sitting on a sycamore branch near the creek. "Pow! Got ya!" Russell whispered.

"I *know* you're not aiming at me." Uncle Bron was looking at him from between his legs. "Something told me I shouldn't have bought that thing for you."

As Russell lowered the slingshot, his fingers slipped and the rock whizzed over Uncle Bron's head. It hit the branch where the squirrel sat. The squirrel leaped from the sycamore toward the weeping willow, missed its mark, and landed on Uncle Bron's back.

Uncle Bron yelled and jumped around in the water. The squirrel scrambled up to Uncle Bron's head and perched there. Uncle Bron looked like he was wearing a squirrel-tail cap. Ducking Uncle Bron's flailing arms, the squirrel skittered down the front of his shirt, fell in the water chattering, and splashed away.

Russell shoved the slingshot back in his pocket. "Sorry, Uncle Bron."

Uncle Bron charged out of the creek. A leaf was stuck to his nose. "Didn't I say put that thing up?" he hollered. "You better straighten up and fly right or you'll never make ten! I tell you one thing and you do the opposite! And didn't I say to keep out of the deep water? Being in this creek's not like sitting in the bathtub, boy! You could step in a deep hole, go down ten or fifteen feet, and I'd never find you. Didn't I say not to shoot at animals? Didn't I say stick with tin cans? Oh, I give up. Come on, we're going home."

Russell waded out of the creek. "It was an accident, honest. Are you gonna tell Mom?"

"What do you think? You made your move. Now you got to pay the price. You're more hard-headed than your daddy, and that's goin' some. Now come on." Slapping at mosquitoes, Uncle Bron stamped through the weeds toward his riding mower for the trip back to the farmhouse.

Russell sat down on a stump. Man, he was in trouble now. First he'd have to listen to Mom fuss at him. Mom didn't care for Uncle Bron fishing with his hands in the first place. She said it was too dangerous. And she liked it even less that Russell wanted to. She'd tell Dad—who was working on oil rigs over in Kuwait—the next time he called. Russell would have to listen to Dad's sermon about responsibility. And it would go on and on and on.

Russell stared glumly at the water and brushed a deerfly away from his face. None of this would have happened if Uncle Bron had just gone ahead and caught a fish like he usually did. Or let him try today.

Russell couldn't help but grin. He didn't know that squirrels could swim. The one that fell off Uncle Bron's head sure did, though.

Suddenly Russell noticed a swirl in the water in front of him. Something was swimming toward the concrete pilings. And it was big.

An idea hit him. If he dragged home a trophy catfish all by himself, Uncle Bron would forget to tell Mom about the slingshot business. They'd both be so pleased and impressed with his catch they'd forget that Russell wasn't supposed to be hand fishing yet anyway.

Instead of following his uncle home, Russell stepped

into the water. Here the water was a little cooler, which meant that it was also deeper. Quickly he was in up to his knees. Holding on to the branches of the sycamores and willows lining the creek, Russell slopped through the muddy water to the pile of concrete slabs.

Russell knew what to do. First you felt around in the water until you found a hole. You stuck your fingers into that hole and felt around for a smooth, bony head and a firm, rubbery mouth without getting stabbed by the catfish's sharp fins. Next you eased your thumb into the catfish's mouth, while your other fingers gripped one side of its gills. Sometimes you had to let it chew on your thumb like it was bait before you could get your thumb in far enough. Finally, you tightened your fingers around the mouth and gills. That was that old McCutcheon Clutch. You dragged that old catfish out of the hole and threw him up on the bank. Ted Carskadon told him so.

When you did it wrong, the catfish—or whatever you had hold of—got away. Sometimes with part of your thumb. But when you did it right, you had yourself a big catfish and a fine meal.

Russell bent and reached into the water with his right hand. Creek water splashed into his mouth. "Yuck." He spit out the muddy water and rubbed a handful of mosquitoes from his face and neck.

He didn't have much time. It would be dark soon.

Then the big mosquitoes, the bloodsuckers, would be all over him. Not to mention snakes and lizards and maybe even bears. Russell paused, remembering the copperhead he'd seen earlier. Maybe he ought to go on home and take his punishment. Maybe Uncle Bron would even be calmed down by now.

He decided to try it one more time, slower. He reached down again, more carefully this time, searching for crevices in the slippery concrete. Nothing. Just as he was about to call it quits, he thought he felt something move under his left hand. He caught his breath. His heart beat faster.

His fingers touched something sharp. A fin? Carefully he poked around some more, this time with his thumb. The water rose up to his pants pockets. Something gave way under his thumb and closed around it, like a baby sucking on a pacifier. And pulled.

Russell gasped and jerked back. Then he grinned. That sure must be what it felt like to have a catfish on. With his other hand, he slapped at the mosquitoes. He'd be full of mosquito bites, but he'd have himself a trophy fish!

He'd let that fish suck a little more, then he'd put the McCutcheon Clutch on him and pull him out. Russell's back began to ache from being bent over for so long. His neck throbbed from having to hold his face up above the water. His cheeks itched from gnat and black-fly bites. He blinked hard to keep the gnats from crawling into his eyes. He snorted to keep them from flying up his nose.

It was time. Russell's fingers scraped against something hard, but he couldn't get a grip. When he tried to pull his hand and his catch out of the water, he couldn't. Instead, whatever had hold of his thumb pulled back.

"Hey!" Russell gasped. This was a big one.

It could be a fifty-pound flathead, or even the one that got away with Uncle Bron's thumb.

Sweat rolled down Russell's face. The water swishing around his hips was colder. When something brushed against his left leg, he jumped. Was that a copperhead? He'd forgotten all about snakes.

"Uncle Bron?" he called out. "You still around anywhere? Uncle Bron? Uncle Bron!"

Only the crickets in the darkness responded. Russell wrestled with the thing that held him captive, but pulling didn't help. His thumb was stuck in the mouth of a monster flathead, and it wouldn't stay where it was forever. Any time now, that fish might decide to move, and when it did, Russell knew he would have to move with it. He did not dare to think where it might go, and where he would have to follow.

"Uncle Bron, it's got me!" Russell screamed. If only

he had followed Uncle Bron back home like he was supposed to . . .

Glancing around at the shadowy trees and bushes, Russell thought he saw two pairs of yellow eyes staring at him. Wolves? Mountain lions? He'd never heard of any mountain lions in Nutbrush County, but that didn't mean they weren't there.

He jerked and pulled and splashed about in the water. He reached down with his other hand to free himself, but he couldn't bend down far enough without getting water in his mouth. He held his breath, closed his eyes, and plunged down into the water and grappled and searched, but he had to come back up for air quickly. And his thumb stayed stuck.

Tears mingled with the creek water on Russell's bug-bitten face. "Momma! Somebody help!"

If he ever, ever, *ever* got out of this predicament, he would never, never, *never* go hand fishing again. He would never tease Uncle Bron again. He'd sit quiet in church, he'd do his homework, and he'd turn off his TV promptly at nine o'clock, just like Mom told him to.

Russell made all the promises he could think of, but still nothing happened. When he heard a rustle in the grass he knew it had to be a bear.

"Ahhhhhhhhhhhhhhhh!"

Something hollered back, "Russell!"

Mom! Sneezing in relief, Russell began to holler. And when the urge to use the bathroom hit him, he didn't try to hold it back. After all, he was in the water anyway.

"Russell, we're coming!" That was Uncle Bron.

Soon Uncle Bron was in the water with him, and Mom was standing on the bank asking if he was all right.

"Mom, it's got me. It's a big ole flathead," Russell gasped. "And I wanted to surprise you and then you wouldn't be mad because I hit Uncle Bron with my slingshot, and I'm really, really, really sorry."

"Just stop your snotting," Uncle Bron said, helping Russell pull at whatever had grabbed hold of him. "I hadn't said a word to her about nothing. If you'd come on back with me you'd have been all right and she'd've never known."

"Wait a minute, I got him!" Russell twisted up his fist and his arm moved free. He brought his hand up toward the surface. "Oh man, here it is!"

Mom shone the lantern on his hand. What they saw was Russell's thumb stuck in the mouth of a five-gallon bleach bottle. Russell stared at the bottle. Uncle Bron put his hand over his mouth and coughed.

"You mean I about got bit to death by mosquitoes and gnats and bears just to catch a dang bottle?" said Russell.

"It musta been stuck between some pieces of concrete," Uncle Bron said after he straightened up. "I bet that's why you couldn't pull it out. Every time you pulled, I bet the current swept it back between the rocks. Till now."

"Don't you guys tell *nobody* about this, okay?" Russell said. His mother reached out her hand to help him to the bank. When he stretched his free arm out, he slipped and fell into the water.

"Yeow!" A sharp pain pricked him in the behind. When he tried to stand up, something heavy pulled him back down in the water by his pants. "Momma!" He knew that copperhead had sunk its poisonous fangs into him now.

"Hold on there, son," said Uncle Bron as he plunged his hands down into the creek beneath Russell. "What—gee-mo-nee! Why, now I've seen it all. Russell, you got him by the seat of your pants. Hold on to'im!"

"Ow, it's biting me!" Russell grabbed at the thing that was attacking him. It was smooth, scaly, and wiggling like crazy. He craned his neck to see—a catfish!

Russell, Uncle Bron, the bleach bottle, and the catfish made it safely to the creek bank.

"Talk about dumb luck," said Uncle Bron. "You caught that fish by the dorsal fin. It musta got snagged on your pants when you fell on it."

Uncle Bron pulled down Russell's pants while his mother focused the lantern on him. "You're not even bleeding," she said, "but I bet it stings. I'll put something on it when we get home, okay?"

"It's not supposed to hurt to catch a fish," Russell said, rubbing his throbbing rear end.

His mother wrapped her sweater around Russell's shoulders when he began to shiver in the cool summer night air. "It hurts the fish, though," she said quietly.

"Now how am I gonna get this bottle off my thumb?" he said.

"Might have to cut your thumb off," Uncle Bron replied. "No, son, I'll cut the bottle off when we get you back home."

"Young man, you know you're in it deep now, and I don't mean water," Mom said. "You had us scared to death. You could have drowned trying to catch that fish."

"Yeah. But I guess it caught me, hunh." Russell nudged the flopping catfish on the bank with his wet shoe a couple times until it rolled down the embankment, fell into the creek, and disappeared.

"Now that was an honorable thing to do," said Uncle Bron, and patted his shoulder.

"You guys promise not to tell how I caught that thing," said Russell.

"What? You mean I can't tell nobody that you caught a bottle fish?" said Uncle Bron. "Why, you just caught one of the same kind that got away from me when I was a kid. We won't tell, son. I fell down in the water, too. I had to learn the hard way. I guess hard heads can make *two* soft behinds."

Never Leave Your Pocketbook on the Floor

Miz Zip shouldn't blame me for all the creepy stuff that happened at school last Friday. She should point that finger at Draculonius Vamp, too.

Friday had started out normal enough. I was at my desk in Miz Sparrow's room at Good Bend K–5 Elementary, with a piece of Gurdy's Greasy Grape Groaners Squirt Gum under my tongue, as usual. Miz Sparrow turned on the TV so we could see *Good Morning, Good Bend Elementary News*, "Live from Charleston, South Carolina," our in-school TV show. As usual.

My twin sister, Moniqua, was anchor. She and her news team gave us the Almanac (the day's date and weather), the Brain Drainer (the daily puzzle), the Slop Bucket (the lunch menu), and the Happenings (special events). While we waited for the show to start, Miz Sparrow let us talk quietly.

"So, Shaniqua, what's our Thought for the Day gonna be?" Kikita whispered to me. Kikita and I were best friends.

"Oh, probably something like 'Don't count your chickens before they hatch,' or 'Always let your smile be your umbrella.' Now, is that wack or what? I don't have any chickens! And to have a smile that big you'd have to have a head the size of a door. Thought for the Day never makes sense."

"Sure doesn't," Kikita said. "Miz Zip said it would make us have values and character and not be slobs."

"But we're fifth-graders!" I stuck out my chest, waggled my head, and giggled. I tried to keep it under control, though, because sometimes when I start giggling, I can't stop. "We already got good character. Plus, I'm lovable, got brains, and I'm cute. Miz Zip's thoughts are for the little kids."

"Girl, you're crazy," Kikita said. "Quit giggling before we get in trouble."

Miz Zip was our principal. She was always on the show. She'd give us the Thought for the Day in her little squeaky voice. She sounded like that black lady in the movie *Gone With the Wind*. She'd just started these Thought things last month, and so far, boy, were they corny!

To me, having a Thought was just one more of Miz Zip's gazillion school rules for me to have to put up with. I understood rules, and I did try to follow them all. Well, most of them. I bet she had me in mind when she thought up the first five rules:

No running or yelling in school except in gym or on the playground.

No weapons, toys, radios, or other music-making devices at any time anywhere on school grounds.

No fighting or unauthorized singing, dancing, or noise-making of any kind anywhere on school grounds.

No unauthorized chewing gum or eating candy or food at any time anywhere except at lunch in the cafeteria.

Clean white Good Bend school-issued uniform shirts and clean blue Good Bend school-issued uniform pants, shorts, or skirts must be worn at all times during school hours and at school activities.

And on and on and on . . .

I glanced at the Rule Book Demerits chart hanging above our dinosaur diorama. By my name were four unhappy faces. Four demerits. After five demerits, Miz Zip called your parents. After ten, she made your parents come to school for a conference and you got placed on the Official Warnings list. There were three Official Warnings, which all carried punishments. After two more demerits, you got Official Warning Punishment point A, which gave you after-school work detention for one hour for five straight days.

Last year I got one week detention for slapping the snot out of a girl who'd thrown my new mittens into a toilet with Number Two in it. Miz Zip made her fish my mittens out, though. She got detention, too. My daddy is a parole officer and Momma works at the Department of Social Services, so they had a fit when they had to come in. Their daughter Shaniqua getting in trouble, again? Moniqua never got in trouble. But I did.

Second Official Warning, point B, was two weeks of after-school work detention. Miz Zip made your folks come in again, and you faced suspension or transfer. Third Official Warning, point C, was so bad nobody knew what it was. I heard that Miz Zip took you down-town to the school board office, where the superintendent pulled out your fingernails and toenails, stapled your lips together, poured syrup all over you, sealed you inside a steel barrel full of scorpions, ants, and maggots, and dropped you by helicopter into the Atlantic Ocean.

Obviously, Miz Zip's rule book and that barrel hung over my head like pterodactyls all day long, because I loved to jump, scream, sing, squeal, dance, get loud, get my clothes reasonably dirty—and chew me some

Gurdy's Greasy Grape Groaners Squirt Gum! I chewed gum in school even though I wasn't supposed to, and when I had to get rid of it in a hurry, I stuck it under my desk or the cafeteria tables. We all did.

When Moniqua's face filled the TV screen again, I sat up. "We're back with part two. Breaking news!" she said. "Miz Zip just handed me an announcement. The famous mystery writer, Mr. Draculonius Vamp, is going to visit with all of the fifth grade this morning in the cafeteria."

My mouth fell open and we all went, "Ohhhh!" I would have jumped out of my chair and cheered, too, but that wasn't allowed. As it was, Miz Sparrow had to snap her fingers and point to the demerits chart to quiet us down and hear what else Moniqua said. Everybody loved Draculonius Vamp's books. We'd just spent the last two weeks reading his book *Fried Shark and Other Culinary Delights*. Another book, about a kid who had a circus living in his head, was called *There's an Elephant Standing on My Eyeballs*.

Miz Zip's face came on the screen next, but then the TV went dead. That happened a lot. Miz Sparrow jiggled the knobs, then shrugged. "Closed circuit short-circuited again," she said. "I guess we won't have a Thought today."

Instead we got ready for Mr. Vamp's visit. Moniqua got

back to class in time to help. Miz Sparrow and I took down the six-foot-long brown papier-mâché shark our class had designed in art last week. It hung from the ceiling. The shark was supposed to be blue, but our art teacher, Miz Jordan, had run out of blue paper. She just said, "Well, we'll use what we got till we get what we want," which is what Miz Zip also likes to say. She said she heard it from Reverend Jesse Jackson. The shark lay on an oval papier-mâché platter with red catsup, yellow mustard, and white tartar sauce spilled over its back. Kikita, Bunchy, and some other kids carried it to the cafeteria. We wanted Mr. Vamp to see it.

While Miz Sparrow was busy, I stuck my hand down in my book bag, which was on the floor under my chair. I needed a new squirt of gum. Pretending to cough, I slipped the gum into my mouth and slowly sucked the juice out. Nobody saw me do it, either. Well, Moniqua did across the room. We could read each other's minds. Her weakness was M&M's, but only one pack a week. I went through two or three pieces of gum every day.

The first thing I saw when my class marched into the cafeteria were three long tables covered with trays of cookies, cake squares, a punch bowl, and two big bouquets of flowers. The next thing I saw was our shark hanging above the stage. Miz Jordan and some boys were hanging up signs that read WELCOME, MR. DRACULONIUS VAMP.

I raised my hand for permission to speak. "I hope that food's for us," I told Miz Sparrow.

Miz Sparrow shook her head. "It's for the superintendent of schools and the teachers from other schools who're coming to hear Mr. Vamp. Sorry."

We all groaned, and Miz Sparrow had to hush us up. Everyone sat down at the cafeteria tables at the front of the room. With my tongue I carefully dug out my gum from where I'd pushed it down between my cheek and back teeth. While rubbing my face with my hands, I rolled that gum around in my mouth and sucked on it. Good thing I had my gum. I was starving! I tucked it back for later.

Under our shark stood Miz Zip, smiling as big as that umbrella she'd told us about. Miz Zip was cool. She still wore her hair in an Afro style. I got to know her real well when I was on detention last year. She didn't have any kids. She said we were her kids. She liked to laugh, but when she got serious, she'd speak real slow in that squeaky voice. Then she'd add real fast, "Seem Sane?" or "Nome Sane?" or "Yunnus Tan?" "Seem Sane?" meant "Do you see what I'm saying?" "Nome Sane?" meant "Do

you know what I'm saying?" "Yunnus Tan?" meant
"Do you understand?" We better say "Yes ma'am"
every time.

Miz Zip hooked a microphone onto the collar of a tall,
thin man. He had a long yellow beard on his face and a
thick yellow braid curling down his back. When he
turned around, the sequined sharks on his fuzzy red
baggy pants and matching shirt sparkled. His fingernails
were painted my favorite color—purple. The brim of his
big flat red hat covered one of his eyes. His other blue
eye stared straight at me and winked. I didn't know what
else to do, so I winked back.

"That's *gotta* be Mr. Draculonius Vamp," Kikita whispered, barely moving her lips. "He dresses crazier than
his name. Look at those big feet!"

"So? He doesn't have to write with his feet," I whispered back. When I noticed Miz Zip looking at me, I
gave her a quick nod to show I hadn't meant to talk so
loud. I sure didn't want another demerit. I sat up straight
so she could see I was behaving.

Miz Zip strolled to the podium. "Good morning,
children."

"Good morning, Miz Zippleton," we said back to her.

"Our visitor today is a famous author, Mr. Draculonius
Vamp, who has written over fifty award-winning books.
Mr. Vamp happened to be in our area for a conference at

the community college. When he heard that Good Bend was one of the top twenty-five K–5 schools in the state, he wanted to visit us. We're just thrilled! It goes to show that 'Patience is a virtue.' Isn't this amazing?"

"Yes ma'am," we said.

"So let's give him our undivided attention, and a Good Bend welcome!"

We stood up and applauded. I shot my hand up to my mouth like I was hiding another cough, sucked out my gum, chewed it twice, and tucked it back.

"That gum is strong, girl," Kikita told me as we sat down. "You better dump it before Miz Sparrow gets a whiff. You know what Miz Zip's rule is about gum, even if we are in the cafeteria."

"And here's what Auntie Marian said she used to tell Daddy when she got tired of him bossing her around when they were little," I whispered. "'I don't care what Brother don't allow, I'm gonna do it anyhow.' And that's what I say about that ole gum rule."

Kikita giggled behind her hand, shook her head, then opened her mouth a little. I could see a roll of gum in there. Keeping an eye on Miz Zip and Miz Sparrow, we slapped hands, coughed, and chewed.

Mr. Vamp left his books on the podium, then stood right in front of me and Kikita. I broke out into a sweat. Had he seen us chewing? When he stretched out his arms, his floppy sleeves made him look like a fuzzy red moth about to land on me. He was so close that I looked right up into his left nostril—and spotted a big booger. Please, Mr. Vamp, I prayed, don't sneeze!

"Youuuu knoooow that you must nevah, evah, evah, *evah* disobey your parents and your teachers," he began in a deep twangy voice. "Because if you *dooo*, bad things can happen to you. Like they did to Luke in my story 'The Last Ten Seconds Before *Kaboom!*'"

When he said *"Kaboom!"* all the lights in the cafeteria went out. Everybody around us laughed and gasped in the dark. Kiki and I grabbed each other and screamed. It was fun! Then the lights came back on. Mr. Vamp stood at the podium smiling at us. "Now that I have your attention," he said, "let me tell you more about my books."

Which he did. He even let us ask him questions. We already knew everything about his books, since we'd read them. But we asked him so many questions about his clothes that Miz Zip finally told us to ask him about other stuff.

I thought of something and raised my hand. "Mr. Vamp, sir, what is your Thought for the Day?" I asked. "We didn't get one from Miz Zip-pleton this morning 'cause the TV went off."

"Thought for the Day?" he said. Miz Zip explained

about the Thought. "Oh, I see," he said. "Here's one: 'Never leave your pocketbook on the floor.'"

I stared at him. Right then I realized that grown folks think up stuff just to mess with us kids. Like Momma's Booger Man. When I was a little kid, Momma said the Booger Man would get me in my bed if I kept acting up. I'd wake up at two o'clock in the morning so scared I'd sneak out of my room and sleep in the bathtub with the light on. Moniqua, who thought it was funny, didn't tell me for a month that the Booger Man was just make-believe.

"Never leave your pocketbook on the floor?" I repeated it, and then I began to giggle. Well, you know about me and giggling. Remembering how it felt trying to sleep in the bathtub made me giggle some more. But this time my giggling got away from me, and I giggled so hard that I got the hiccups. Real loud ones. Well, that got everybody else laughing at me. Miz Zip had been smiling. But her smile faded away when we kept laughing, and I kept on hiccuping. Bunchy behind me slapped me on the back to make me stop hiccuping. And right then my gum slipped down my throat.

The next thing I knew, Miz Zip was in front of me. She clapped her hand over my mouth. "Enough, Miss Shaniqua Godette, enough," she said quietly. Her eyes had gone to little squints. She added soft and quick, "Yell like that again and you get five demerits. Nome Sane? Yunnus Tan?"

Bug-eyed, I nodded. When she removed her hand, she had my slobber on it.

Mr. Vamp stood by the podium with his arms crossed while Miz Zip got the other kids quieted down. "And where *is* your pocketbook, Shaniqua?" he asked.

"I don't have a pocketbook, Mr. Vamp, sir. I got a book bag," I said. "It's under my desk, on the floor."

Everybody started to laugh again, then shut up quick. "Well, 'Never leave your pocketbook on the floor' sounds strange, but it also makes sense," Mr. Vamp said. "If it's lying on the floor, you never know what might crawl into it. Where do you think I get my book ideas from? From old sayings like that. Those sayings all just mean that you should use your common sense."

"Yes sir," I said. "Thank you." But inside I said to myself that I was right. Miz Zip's Thoughts for the Day were all just make-believe, like Mr. Vamp's books and Momma's Booger Man.

Afterwards, when we stood in line to get Mr. Vamp's autograph, I realized I didn't have my autograph book. Miz Sparrow let me go back to our classroom to get it. I rushed to my desk and, unbuckling the top flap of my bag, pulled out my autograph book.

Suddenly, *whoosh!* My book bag—get this—*flew* from my hands and out the door! Instead of the two side pockets where I kept my pens, pencils, and calculator, there were two large brown leathery wings! Instead of a top flap and handle, there was a brown leathery triangular head on a long scrawny neck. The beak was orange, and it was made of two of my Number One lead pencils, long and sharp.

"Hey, c'mere!" I rushed after it, but it flew into the cafeteria.

Squawking, this thing—this bird-bag—flapped over Mr. Vamp's head to our shark and perched on its snout. Then it swooped down toward me, clacking its beak. When I ducked under a cafeteria table, it landed on the seat next to me and stared at me with its beady buckle eyes. I froze. Suddenly it whipped its snaky neck around and swung its head under the table toward me. I scrambled on my hands and knees away from it and screamed for Miz Zip.

But Miz Zip just stood there and said, "Miss Shaniqua Godette, one demerit for unauthorized running, Norne Sane? One demerit for unauthorized noisemaking, Yunnus Tan?"

The bird-bag flew at me, but I ducked again. It landed on the reception table, knocked over the punch bowl, and ended up in the cake tray. Sticky strawberry juice and yellow frosting splattered all over a man whose badge said SUPERINTENDENT.

I crouched under another table and licked frosting off my hands. Just then I noticed gobs of purplish putty dripping down from beneath the table where I hid. It smelled just like Gurdy's Greasy Grape Groaners Squirt Gum. How could that be?

As the drops hit the floor, they formed a large purple puddle that began to ooze toward me. The sticky purple ooze crawled onto my shoes and up my legs. One fell on my hand and inched up my arm. It felt like a snail.

"Miz Zip!" I yelled, slapping the gum away. Another gob leaped on my ear and tried to crawl inside it, then headed for my mouth. I clapped my hands over my mouth, but the gum forced its slimy body between my lips. It tasted like cottage cheese left in the refrigerator for six months. It filled my mouth so fast that I couldn't talk. All I could do was gurgle for help. My own gum was holding me hostage!

"Phelvh! Miv Viff, phelvh!"

I staggered out from under the table with a slimy mountain of greenish purple, moldy Gurdy's Greasy Grape Groaners Squirt Gum clinging to me. Kikita, Miz Zip, Bunchy—everybody stared. Nobody helped. I wished I had never ever chewed gum in my life.

Then out of the one eye that I could still see with, I

saw the bird-bag pull itself out of the cake. When it spied me, it clacked its beak and lurched toward me. In a second it was only inches away, with its beak aimed right at my head. With my last bit of strength, I drew my left arm up to protect my face. I took a deep breath and screamed as loud as I could, "Pffelpf! Pffelpf!"

"Quit fighting, Shaniqua, and lay still!"

"Get that thing away from me!" I screamed. "Get back, or else I'll bop you one!"

When I opened my eyes, I saw Moniqua hanging on to my left arm and Miz Zip hanging on to my right. Mr. Vamp stood behind her. I lay on a kindergartner's sleeping mat on the cafeteria floor. The other fifth-graders, the superintendent, and the teachers were gone. And so was the mountain of Gurdy's Greasy Grape Groaners Squirt Gum.

"Honey, you passed out after you were hiccuping," Miz Zip said. She unfolded some tissue paper. My big wad of gum lay in the middle of it. "You choked on some gum. You just now spit it out. Are you all right?"

"Yes ma'am," I whispered. I wiped at my mouth. It had a sour-grapes taste. "Is that bird-bag gone?"

"What bird-bag?" said Miz Zip.

I tried to tell them what happened, but Moniqua gave

me a look that meant "Shut up, don't make things worse."

"I bet I got two million demerits now, hunh?" I said to Miz Zip. I saw myself being stuffed into that barrel with those ants and maggots for breaking so many rules.

"You don't have two million demerits, Miz Shaniqua, but you sure got a lot more than you had before. Honey, you could have choked to death on all that gum! Let this be a lesson to you. There's a reason why we have rules in this world. You know what our Good Bend rule book says."

I sure did. I also knew that I'd probably have to stay after school for the next zillion years picking off every dang piece of gum I'd stuck all over the place. From where I was on the floor I saw lots of wads poking out from under cafeteria tables and seats. I wasn't sure, but it looked like one of them moved.

"I guess maybe you won't leave your pocketbook on the floor anymore, will you?" said Mr. Vamp.

I shook my head. "I sure won't. And I even got my own Thought for the Day: 'Never stick your Gurdy's where it ain't supposed to be.'"

Don't Split the Pole

As soon as Lizard heard Mrs. Gillikin's first screech, he thrashed his way up out of her patch of prickly hollyhock flowers. He snatched his skateboard and sped after his older brother, Dart. As he rolled down Fisher Street, Lizard glanced back. Mrs. Gillikin stood on her porch by her orange garbage bag pumpkin and her wooden witch. She was shaking her fist and yelling, just like last time.

First Lizard felt over his left arm. Then he checked his right. No broken bones. That was a relief. Since last year, when he started skateboarding, he'd broken his right collarbone and the middle and pinky fingers on his left hand, and he'd had four stitches in his left calf. He hated being so clumsy on his skateboard. Seemed like he fell off more than he stayed on.

He hoped his oversized Carolina Panthers T-shirt and baggy pants were blowing out behind him the way Dart's were, like flags on a pole. He hoped he looked as cool as Dart did, too. Because despite Morehead City's crisp October air, Lizard was so embarrassed about falling in Mrs. Gillikin's flowers again that he had sweated up his temples and the back of his shirt something awful. Having the whole neighborhood hear her screeching at him didn't help, either. Unlike Dart and the rest of Dr. Dart's Ultimate Posse Rollers, Lizard didn't like to have people fuss at him. Especially when he was skateboarding on their property without permission.

He wished he was twelve years old like Dart, instead of only nine. He wished he knew how to say just the right thing and enough of it at the right time, like Dart did. He wished he had curly black hair like Dart's, instead of his own red bushy stuff. Most of all, he wished he was tall and coordinated and had pecs and abs and a cute butt, like the girls said Dart had, instead of being a short and scrawny kid who talked too much and always tripped over everything. He even fell out of bed in the middle of the night.

Half a block later, Lizard caught up with Dart. "Think she'll really call the cops if we skateboard over her driveway again? She was really yelling this time. I bet she calls Mom. She did last time, remember? I can just hear her: 'Miz Willis, Lizario and Dartanyan were playing in my yard again and I want it stopped!' Mom told me she wasn't gonna come pick us up from the police station if the cops ever do take us in."

"Skate or die, Lizario," Dart said. Lizard watched while Dart and his skateboard leaped up to the metal railing bordering the steps of the Morehead City Small Motors Repair Garage, slid down the rail, hit the pavement safely, and stopped.

Lizard took a deep breath. He picked up speed to jump over a sawhorse straddling a pothole in the middle of Fisher Street. At the last minute he swerved around it.

"Lost your nerve, huh, chickenhead?" Dart said.

Lizard frowned. "Don't call me that. Maybe I'll do it next time."

Things would be easier if he had somewhere to really practice. It had been easy to skate around Morehead City until a guy from out of town claimed he got hurt at the city's skateboard lot. Next thing Lizard knew, the city had torn down the ramp. Most stores didn't allow skateboarding in their parking lots, even after hours. Some had NO SKATEBOARDS signs in their windows. And the few stores and streets that didn't seem to mind weren't the ones that the Posse liked. Fisher Street had the last good curbs in town.

Dart and Lizard sailed past a police car in the parking lot of the Dairy Creme. Inside, Lizard saw Sparks, one of Dart's Posse, sitting at a booth with two zit-faced guys that Lizard didn't recognize. Sparks pointed at Dart and said something to the guys, who snickered. Lizard hoped he and Dart wouldn't have to be bothered with Sparks, because Sparks was a pain.

"Sparks is still flapping his lips all over town about how you gave up looking for some place," Lizard hollered to Dart.

Dart shrugged. "Remember what that guy said in *Forrest Gump*? 'Stupid is as stupid does'? That's Sparks. Stupid."

"Yeah, stupid," Lizard agreed. Sparks, who was twelve, was trying to set a record by wearing the same blue-black-and-red lumberjack shirt and holey blue jeans for as long as possible before his mother snatched them off him to be washed. He'd worn them this time for the last four days. From the smell, that had to be a record, Lizard thought. Sparks used to borrow people's skateboards and switch the wheels for himself until Dart found out and threatened to kick him out of the Posse.

Lizard looked back over his shoulder. "Oh geez, here they come," he said.

"Hey, hey, Dart, wait," Sparks hollered. Dart slowed down, sighing. "Mojo and Acer here are from Beaufort," Sparks said. He jerked his thumb at the two zit-faced boys with him. "They know some spots out there where we can roll."

"Yeah, like we're gonna skateboard five or ten miles

round trip to Beaufort every day," Dart said. "Real no-brainer."

"Well, nobody wants to go on Fisher anymore, except you and Lizzy," said Sparks with his face screwed up. "Mojo got his board snatched 'cause he tried to jump Miz Gillikin's dog sleeping in the street and squashed it. She called the cops. I told the Posse we oughta find someplace else and everybody said right on."

"Oh, so you're in charge now, huh?" Dart said.

"Somebody's gotta be." Sparks folded his arms.

"Dart's found a place," Lizard said. "And when he's ready, he'll say where, won't ya, Dart? Huh, Dart. Won't ya, Dart?"

"Yeah, yeah," said Dart. "Later, Sparks." He pushed past Sparks and the other boys. Lizard had to hurry to catch up with him.

Dart rolled his skateboard with his foot through a pile of dead leaves in the gutter as he waited for the cars to pass. His thick eyebrows met in such a furious furry line that it looked like a big black caterpillar had stuck itself on his forehead.

"Are you crazy?" Dart snapped. "We're getting heat about Fisher, Sparks's wolfin' about the Posse, and then you start jawin' that I got another place."

"I had to," said Lizard. "Sparks was making you look

bad. I'm sorry. So c'mon, show me how to jump something, okay?"

"I don't feel like it." Dart stamped off, and Lizard, his feet dragging, followed.

Back home, Lizard leaned against the front-porch pillar watching Dart sit on the carport wall and spin the back wheels of his skateboard with his fingers. Through the window Lizard could see his arithmetic book waiting on the kitchen table, but he knew he couldn't concentrate. "You think Sparks'll take over the Posse?"

Dart snorted. "You know everything. You tell me."

"Well, I've been thinking about what he said about Beaufort."

"Yeah, you can drive us up there in your limo."

"Can't we find something closer, like maybe at that old flea market building? You know, that burned-out building off Highway 70, past the produce market. It's not that far. This girl Marcy gave a report in my social studies class about it when we had to write something on local landmarks. She said it used to be called the Crystal Coast Exchange Flea Market. There's a big parking lot behind it."

Dart stared at Lizard, then smacked his forehead with his palm. "Yes! Yes! C'mon, chickenhead." He grabbed Lizard by the front of his shirt and pulled him behind him. They tucked their skateboards under their arms and headed for their dirt bikes.

After ten minutes of riding, they reached the turnoff to the fenced-in, burned-out Exchange building. Its gate hung open, and Lizard and Dart rode through to a concrete pillar that held up a broken neon sign. The charred skeleton of the long, one-story building gaped at them like blackened teeth. Behind the building they could see portions of the parking lot.

They walked over to a bent-up, pockmarked white sign with a big red arrow on it marked RULES. It was stuck to a green metal pole with another little sign below it.

On the RULES sign it said customers were supposed to pay at the gate, then follow the road and arrow around the pillar to the right to park their vehicles. Then they were supposed to walk into the mall from the back. When they finished shopping, they were supposed to drive out the other way. Walk-ins paid at the gate, too, then followed the same road in and out as the folks who drove. They were *not* to jump the fence or go round the pillar any other way.

Beneath the RULES sign was another small handwritten sign that said: DON'T SPLIT THE POLE—OR ELSE YOU'LL HAVE BAD LUCK!

"So nobody could cheat and get in free," Lizard said. "Or else they'd have bad luck."

Dart walked in past the EXIT pole. Lizard walked in the right way, past the ENTRANCE sign. "There, lookee, Lizard. I just went in the wrong way and didn't pay either. Nothing bad happened."

They walked around to the parking lot. There was an abandoned flatbed trailer back there, along with scattered piles of logs, tires, brown-and-red rusty barrels, and several junk cars and trucks. The parking lot was a large square of concrete bordered by wide patches of weedy dirt. It was perfect.

Dart and Lizard did high fives. For the first time that afternoon Lizard saw Dart smile. "This is all right, man!" he said. "This'll be awesome. Nobody'll mess with us here in a hundred years. Thanks." Dart punched him on the shoulder.

"Marcy said this flea market was really popular," Lizard said proudly. "People brought in all kinds of stuff to sell from all around. Then it caught on fire fifteen or twenty years ago. I forget how."

Dart started to pile logs around the lot to make practice jumps. "Now you can build up to jumping over that sawhorse," he told Lizard. "This flatbed trailer'll be the ultimate ramp." He glanced at the end of the building nearest the trailer. The roof was still intact. "We could even jump from the roof to the flatbed. Look at ole redhead Lizard fly through the air like an ole woodpecker."

"Right," Lizard said aloud. *Wrong,* he told himself.
"Let's see what's left inside."

There wasn't much—just waist-high wheat grass growing up through the holes in the wooden floors, a few rusty chairs, pieces of charred wood, and old birds' nests that had fallen from the rafters. By standing in the center of the building, Lizard could see all the way through it. He blinked and squinted. "Hey, Dart, we ain't by ourselves." He pointed to the end. "There's a girl over there."

"Yeah, and she's sellin' cookies and milk," Dart said sarcastically. "No man, your eyes are crooked. That's just weeds and junk."

Watching for snakes, Lizard followed Dart to the end of the building. When they neared the end, they froze. The weeds and junk still looked like a girl—a blond-headed one—wearing a red FISHERMAN'S PARADISE T-shirt and green shorts. She stood behind a heap of something covered by a white sheet with a grin on her face. Like she'd been expecting them.

"Hi, guys. Come get it before the rest of the folks get here," she called out. She pulled the sheet off the table like a bullfighter removing her cape.

Before them sat six aquarium-sized glass cases on two tables. Inside the cases were Civil War–era gold coins and brown paper money, neatly folded Union and Confederate flags, pairs of run-over, beat-up black boots, gray-and-blue soldiers' jackets, and rows of ancient rifles, pistols, and bullets.

Lizard's blue eyes bugged. The girl looked familiar. "Wha—What's this stuff? What're you doing? Where'd this stuff come from? Who are you?"

"I'm sellin' my uncle's Civil War memorabilia, whadja think?" she replied. "This is a flea market, 'member? Who're *you?*"

Without answering, Lizard reached out a trembling right forefinger and touched the case. It was real, all right.

"Don't do that," the girl said. "Uncle Harker has a hissy fit when folks go pecking and poking like that. But if there's a particular thing you want to see up close, I can bring it out. He don't much like too many people handling his stuff, 'cause folks'd steal it in a minute. But y'all look like nice guys." She smiled at them. "When Uncle Harker comes back, I'm gonna go help my momma down at table sixteen. She's sellin' tapes."

"Wait a minute." Dart held up his hand. "Are you crazy? This place is closed. It's a dump! Nobody sells any stuff out here anymore! Look back there! Junk! Garbage! Zero! Zilch!"

When he turned around to point out what he meant, his voice stuck in his throat. Lizard looked back, too, and gasped. Behind them were hundreds of people walking around, standing at dozens of tables full of items. The building now looked like it had never caught on fire.

"I'm freakin'," Dart whispered. "Or I'm dreamin', 'cause this ain't real."

"And I'm in your dream tellin' you it ain't real," Lizard croaked, "but it sure doesn't feel like a dream. Let's get outta here!"

"Yeah, you better hurry if you're gonna buy," said the girl, "because it'll get real busy in a few minutes. You're getting an advance peek. My name's Gloria Dawn. What's y'all's?"

"D-D-Dart and Lizard," said Dart. He backed away from Gloria Dawn. "But we saw everything all messed up just five minutes ago!"

"Maybe so," Gloria Dawn said. She put her hands on her hips and stared at them with eyes so pale blue they looked translucent. "But it sure ain't now, is it?"

Lizard peered into a case full of miniature cars and trucks, tractors, and train cabooses. His eyes riveted on a tiny skateboard that looked a lot like his. Suddenly he realized he was no longer carrying his own board. "Hey, where's my board?" He shook Dart's arm and pointed into the case. "Isn't that it?" he whispered. "And yours too! How'd they get in there?"

"That's impossible, Lizard," said Dart, looking around for his.

"Uncle Harker finds the strangest things." Gloria Dawn set the little skateboards on the table. "They're ten dollars apiece, but I'll sell 'em to ya for seven."

Lizard picked up one of the boards and turned it over. "See, here's my initials." He grabbed the little skateboards and stuffed them into his baggy pants' side pockets. "I don't know how your uncle got 'em, but I'm takin' 'em back." He turned away from Gloria Dawn and found himself staring at the gray uniform of a frowning man with a beard. The man's hands were pressed against the sword and pistol strapped to his belt.

"Uncle Harker, they were just looking. They weren't doing nothing," Gloria Dawn said.

"Of course not. What'd you put in your pants, kid? Aha! Caught ya! A thief always returns to the scene of the crime." He drew his pistol and grabbed at Lizard's pocket.

Lizard and Dart flew. They pushed around the clumps of people who had begun to gather at the sound of Uncle Harker's shouts. Lizard banged into a woman with a bulging plastic sack and knocked it to the floor. Towels, handkerchiefs, and men's underwear flew everywhere.

"'Scuse me," Lizard said. Dart snatched Lizard to his feet. They fled from that hall into another, searching for an exit.

"Go, go, go!" Dart shouted. He swerved down an aisle full of produce. When a man holding a head of lettuce in each hand jumped into the middle of the aisle with his arms outstretched to block their way, Dart ducked under one elbow, Lizard under the other. Lizard's foot, though, skidded on a leaf of lettuce, and he fell into a tub of tomatoes on the floor. Smash! Tomato juice dripped off his nose and ears, and crushed chunks clung to his red hair. Dodging the spidery fingers of the screaming woman vendor bearing down on him, Lizard scrambled away to another hallway.

Where was Dart? Had someone grabbed him? Lizard panted, biting his lip. He spied Uncle Harker in the next aisle over, waving his arms and shouting. A woman pointed Lizard's way. Frantically Lizard glanced around, then shot off in the opposite direction. He slipped around shoppers at green bean and yellow corn stands, upset a squash cart, and bumped over a table of cabbage and zucchini.

Lizard's lungs were on fire, and his nose was running faster than his legs. His heart pounded so fast he thought it would jump up his throat and out his mouth. He also had to pee.

He zipped around a corner by the crochet and sewing displays and sped down another hallway. Dart! With relief, he ducked after his brother under some canvas covering a table in an empty booth. "What're we gonna do?" Lizard whispered, his throat so dry that the words almost stuck in his mouth. "That Harker dude's gonna shoot us for sure."

"Yeah, chickenhead, 'cause you stole his stuff. What'd you expect?"

"But they're ours!" Lizard pulled a skateboard from his pocket. "Feel your initials there, scratched on the bottom?"

"Geez, you're right. Let me think a minute, Lizzy."

Voices grew louder and closer; then there was shouting. Lizard's eyes and nose burned. "What's that smell?"

Dart peeked out from a slit in the canvas. "Oh Lord, the whole hallway's fulla smoke, Lizzy. The building's on fire! We gotta move!"

"How? Where?"

"I don't know. I only saw two exits, and Harker was near one of 'em. I don't know where the other one is from here. But we can't stay here." Dart crept out from under the table.

Taking a deep breath and sending up a prayer to the Lord to save them, Lizard crawled out after him. Wind-driven smoke billowed up the hallway toward them, along with more screams and shouts. Dart pushed Lizard around to run the other way. They ran into a dead end. The angry voices were closer.

Lizard turned cold. "Dart, I just remembered something about how this flea market caught fire. Marcy said that a man named Harker did it. He thought the flea market owner's kids were stealing stuff from him, but the owner wouldn't do anything about it. They got into a big argument, and then Harker set fire to the place. And you know what, Dart?"

"What, Lizard, what? What else did you just *happen* to remember now that we're gonna die in the middle of a fire?"

"Well, Marcy showed us a newspaper clipping. There were pictures of that girl, Gloria Dawn, and Harker. They died in that fire."

"How could you forget something like that?" Dart squeaked. "Lizzy, this ain't a dream. It's a nightmare. This place is haunted. We'll never get out."

A lone figure charged toward them through the smoke. It was Gloria Dawn. "Y'all follow me," she said as she went past. When they just stood there, she shouted, "Or else let Uncle Harker get ya, one or t'other."

Dart still hesitated. "What are you?" he asked, but she didn't answer.

Lizard, though, ran after her. "Uncle Harker set the flea market on fire, didn't he?" He repeated to her what he remembered about the fire. She darted into another stall, waving at them to hurry. "Yeah, it was Uncle Harker," she finally said over her shoulder. She began pulling on a rope attached to a square in the ceiling.

"Help me get this ladder down," she said. "Uncle Harker tried to put a curse on the people who were stealing. First he put up that 'Don't Split the Pole' sign in the front. He figured people who didn't abide by rules deserved to have bad luck. And he thought that sign would scare them into behaving. But everybody just laughed when they read it and stuff kept getting stolen. Uncle Harker finally figured it was the owner's kids doing the stealing. They had a big argument and Uncle Harker set the place on fire. Everybody was supposed to get out 'cause it started out as just a small fire—and everybody did. But I got trapped. So Uncle Harker came back in for me. We didn't get out. Sometimes trying to do bad things to other people just boomerangs back on you." She tugged on the rope some more.

"I don't get that part about 'Don't split the pole,'" Lizard said.

"Everybody knows it's bad luck for people to split up going around a pole," Gloria Dawn said. "You musta split up coming in. You sprung Uncle Harker's trap. To take off the bad luck you gotta say 'Bread and butter' or throw salt over your shoulder or drink buttermilk or—I forget what else. C'mon, pull! Pull!" They were still trying to get the ladder down.

"You guys got awful bad timing," Gloria Dawn said. "Today's the twentieth anniversary of the fire. Uncle Harker's sure you're the owner's kids. He won't stop till he gets you. Pull harder! Hurry!"

With the last pull, an iron ladder stretched down to them from the ceiling. Gloria Dawn pointed to it. "Get going! Maybe you can find a way to jump off without catching on fire or falling through the roof."

"I ain't goin' up there," Dart said. "We'll be trapped, Lizard."

"But Dart, we're trapped now." Lizard turned back to Gloria Dawn, but she had disappeared into the smoke.

"We ain't got a choice, Dart, unless you got some salt or some buttermilk," Lizard said. He started pulling himself onto the ladder. He looked down at Dart. "C'mon, man, we gotta go!"

When Dart still didn't move, Lizard reached down and yanked him by the hair. "You come on here, you chickenhead!"

Dart looked up with big eyes. "Okay, Lizario," he said. "I'm comin'."

Lizard climbed up the ladder. Dart followed. Lizard felt

his way across the attic boards and saw the sky in a small opening in the roof. He drew in a deep lungful of fresh air. Beneath them, Lizard heard more angry shouts.

Lizard pulled and tugged at the wood to enlarge the opening, but it wouldn't give. More and more smoke seeped up through the attic floor and burned his eyes until he couldn't see. His lungs ached. Dart shouldered him away from the hole and, with his strong hands, pounded at the roof until the wood gave way. He pulled himself up through the hole and then helped Lizard through.

Outside, they could see the flatbed trailer, the junk cars, and the weedy parking lot below. And beneath them were those crazed voices, smoke and flames, and Uncle Harker.

Thumps sounded closer. Lizard drew in another lungful of fresh air. He pulled out his skateboard, yanked the shoelaces from his shoes, tied the laces together, and then strapped the skateboard to his foot with the laces.

"What're you doin', Lizzy? We can climb down the side," said Dart.

"No, we gotta get off here faster than that, else we're gonna get fried. Or Uncle Harker's gonna get us. He's got a whole gang down there now, and they ain't afraid of no fire. They're ghosts, remember? We gotta do some-thing now."

"No, wait, Lizzy!" Dart screamed.

But Lizard pushed off with his free foot and hurtled down the roof on his other foot, with the skateboard tied to it. He shot out into the sky, his arms behind him, leaning into the air like he'd seen skiers do during the winter Olympics on *ABC Wide World of Sports*. He was an arrow, weightless. Then he began to plunge like a rock, the air ballooning out his shirt. Lizard crashed upright onto the flatbed trailer. He bumped and rolled across the rough surface. As the edge of the flatbed rushed toward him, Lizard tried to brake with his other foot. Covering his head with his arms, Lizard skidded off the trailer and hit the ground. Hard.

When Lizard opened his eyes, he saw the silhouette of the burned-out Crystal Coast Exchange before him in the pink-blue twilight of the evening sky. The smell of smoldering leaves thickened the air. When he slowly sat up, sparks of fire shot through his right shoulder. He saw Dart sprawled on his back in the weeds, looking at him. Lizard got to his hands and knees and began to crawl toward his brother, fearful.

"Dart, you all right? Dart, say something, man."

"Hey, man. That was awesome, what you did," Dart

said. "You should have seen yourself. Perfect form—like an eagle. I ain't never gonna call you chickenhead again. You okay?"

Lizard let himself back down to the ground and rubbed his shoulder. "Feels like I knocked my collarbone out again. I don't think I'll be afraid of jumping over a dumb old sawhorse anymore. I can't believe I jumped off a roof on an itsy bitsy skateboard. Was I really awesome? What'd you think when you jumped?"

"Jump? Hey, I ain't crazy. That's why I was hollering at you. There was a metal fire escape right by where we were. I climbed down."

Lizard stared at him, and then they both began to laugh so hard that Lizard had to stop to keep his shoulder from hurting so bad.

"Lizzy, you know that Gloria Dawn we were talking to was a ghost, don't you?"

"I don't know nothing," Lizard said, "but that I jumped off a roof onto a flatbed trailer and didn't break every bone in my body. None of the Posse'll believe us. I wish somebody had videotaped that because I sure ain't gonna do it again."

"Yeah, my heart about stopped when you went over. Mom'll kill us both if she finds out. Maybe we better chill out from skateboarding till you heal up. We can just go on down to the Seafood Festival this weekend and get into the Flounder Fling or some other stuff. Maybe we can ask Reverend Logsdon at church if he'll let us use the parking lot for skateboarding when he knows it's gonna be empty."

Lizard stared up at the darkening sky. He thought he saw more stars beginning to peek out. When he was up there in the air it had seemed like he could almost touch them. "Hey, Dart, let's tell Sparks and those two zitheads that we got a new place. Tell 'em to come out here. But tell 'em that they gotta split the pole first to get in."

Big Things Come in Small Packages

I want to tell you about a boy I knew who lived in Morehead City, North Carolina, some years ago named Tucker Willis. He lived by Calico Creek where it narrows down to marsh grass, flounder, and fiddler crabs. It's not far from the back side of the Morehead City Port Terminal, where the big ships come in from the Atlantic Ocean.

Everybody liked him, and he was good at almost everything he put his hand to. But when Tucker turned eleven or twelve, he was still so short he looked like an elf. And you know how it is when you're a little different from other folks in even some harmless kind of way. Kids called him Tom Thumb, squirt, midget, inchworm, dwarf.

I thought Tucker was the cutest little thing in the world. But to him back then I was ole knock-kneed LaShana Mae, the girl who lived down the street. I was a couple years younger than him. We were friends, though, and went to the same church—St. Luke's Missionary Baptist—and the same school.

Back in those days, in the 1970s, young boys and girls didn't hang out as boyfriend and girlfriend like kids do now. Plus, I was just a skinny girl with braids and braces. Kids called me Wires because of those braces, and boy, did it ever make me mad! So Tucker and I had a lot in common, and lots of times we talked about the things kids called us, especially when we went fishing.

Even though being called those names hurt, Tucker gave up fighting the kids who said them. Fighting didn't help. The name-callers were all too big for him to beat up. So after a while, he learned to ignore the teasing. Most times he laughed it off. He was a tough little dude. But oh mercy, how he hated those names!

One day Tucker did something that made everybody stop calling him names he didn't like. I think it helped him grow a few inches, too.

You need to know a few things about this boy before I tell you what changed things around. Tucker could do almost anything that any other kid his age could do. He was a hotshot shortstop on the Little League baseball team. He could jump like a flea on the basketball court. He was smart in school. He was in the Boy Scouts. He could swim like a fish—and even surf!

He looked like a Tootsie Roll to me in that big ocean. Yeah, I had a name for him, too. I called him Tootsie Roll, but never to his face. I just kept it to myself. And when I called him that in my head, I didn't mean it in a bad way.

Tucker could do some fishing. He especially liked to fish his folks' little pier alongside their house. In the summertime he'd lie on his stomach on the pier and catch some of the biggest flounder to come out of Calico Creek. Instead of a rod and reel, he used a handful of fishing line, a hook baited with shrimp, and a sinker to keep the bait from floating on the surface.

He'd dangle that shrimp an inch or two off the bottom, right in front of a flounder's nose. Sometimes we'd fish together on his pier, and I wouldn't catch diddly-squat, not even a pinfish, not even a lizard fish, nothing. But ole Tootsie Roll could catch 'em.

I tried fishing the way he did, but most of the time I used a rod and reel 'cause I thought the way Tucker did it was country. I still couldn't catch anything, not in Calico Creek. I did all right when I fished at the pier in Atlantic Beach.

That's how I'd see Tucker surfing. He even got teased about surfing, because not many black kids we knew surfed. Shoot, as much as we all loved the water, not a whole lot of us even knew how to swim. I didn't. Not until Tucker taught me later on.

He and his dad or mom would fish out on their own little pier all night sometimes with a Coleman lantern for light. His folks used regular rods and reels. I never fished out there at night with them because the mosquitoes and the gnats would about eat me up.

Plus, my momma liked to tell me that they used to do baptizing in that creek, which was okay. But then Momma'd say, "LaShana Mae, you watch out about being around that creek by yourself at night. The people who got baptized there and who've passed on come back to that creek as spirits in the middle of the night when the moon's full. They'll be singing and celebrating and shouting and praising, and they don't want to be disturbed. Unless you wanna join in with 'em."

Me being a scared little kid, you can believe that Momma didn't have to worry about me going out to *nobody's* Calico Creek by myself at night. But sometimes I'd go to my window at night and look out to see if anybody was celebrating the way she said. All I ever saw were grown folks fishing. Sometimes somebody would holler when they caught a big one. After I got grown I understood that Momma told me that story to try to help me stay out of trouble. She was worried I'd drown or get into some kind of foolishness. Well, it worked. I knew that it was easy to get into trouble when you're out someplace where you're not supposed to be.

Anyway, what happened to change all the name-calling started when Tucker was on his pier trying to

catch a flounder. He noticed a man standing on the
Moten Motel dock just a few yards from him. The man
had a thick white mustache and Vandyke beard and wore
a blue-and-gold military-style jacket and cap. I wasn't
there, so I didn't see him, but that's what Tucker told me.

When the man waved, Tucker, being a friendly kind of
kid, waved back. They struck up a conversation. The
man said his name was Richard and that he was staying
at the motel for a few days. His home was in Manteo, on
Roanoke Island, not far from the Outer Banks, where he
worked with the U.S. Lifesaving Service.

Tucker figured what he meant was that he was with
the U.S. Coast Guard. Tucker was pretty knowledgeable
about the coast guard, but he had never heard of this lifesaving service. Tucker asked the man if he liked to fish.
Richard said yes. He'd been a commercial fisherman
before he became a captain in the lifesaving service. As a
lifesaver, he said, he and his men went into the ocean in
the middle of hurricanes and nor'easters to save passengers and crew members whose ships were sinking.

Of course, anything about water fascinated Tucker, so
he must have asked this Richard a million questions.
Richard didn't seem to mind, though. He said he didn't
get to talk to kids much anymore.

Richard said a good crewman had to be strong, an
excellent swimmer, a quick thinker, and in good physical

health, have good eyesight, and understand how dangerous the sea can be. He told so many stories about lifesaving that Tucker wished he could enlist right away, and said so. He had the right qualifications—other than being too young, of course. And too short.

Richard told him it wasn't the size of a person that got the job done. It was how bad the person wanted to do it. How were those huge ships two and more stories high able to move into the Morehead City port and back out to sea? Most couldn't do it without little tugboats pushing and pulling them in, Richard said. A tugboat could bring in a ship many times its size.

Richard said that Tucker would make a good tugboat and one day might even grow to be a big ship. He thanked Tucker for the conversation, said maybe they'd meet again, and then the man wandered off back toward the motel. Tucker said for the rest of the afternoon, he thought over what Richard had said.

A few days later, Tucker decided to go with his dad to the Atlantic Beach pier to fish. His daddy worked there as a cook. For some reason I couldn't go that day. I've always wished I had. Tucker said he took his surfboard, too, in case fishing got slow. It was early morning, but a hot July wind blew in from the southwest, making the waves choppy and sandy. The tide was going out. Hardly anybody was on the pier, which was another hint that the fish might not be biting. Tucker said only one guy was in the water, floating on a red raft like a huge jellyfish.

After a good hour had passed and he hadn't got a bite, Tucker left his rod and reel with his father in the pier restaurant's kitchen and went surfing. After he swam out far enough, he climbed onto his surfboard and rode a wave in. When he glanced back at the pier, guess who he saw? His new friend, Richard, on the pier, clapping for him. At least this time he had on shorts and a regular shirt. Tucker said he bet Richard had about burnt up in that heavy uniform the other day.

Richard hollered, "Do it, Tugboat! Pull that ole wave in!"

Tugboat? Tucker said he frowned until he remembered Richard's story about tugboats. So he waved back and swam out to pull in another one, passing the man on the raft. The man said, "You're kinda little to be way out here, ain't ya, squirt?" Tucker just shook his head and kept going.

Tucker pulled in four more waves until he noticed a tall purple thunderhead rising up on the southwest horizon. That cloud meant a storm was probably on its way, but Tucker figured he had at least half an hour before the wind kicked up the waves and blew the cloud in and the rain began. Tucker wasn't afraid of a thing, but his common sense and his folks had told him to always leave away from water when storms and lightning came along. It's hard to get grown without having common sense, because being stupid can get you killed sometimes.

Keeping an eye on the horizon, Tucker went on pulling in those waves until a huge one arched up behind his back and crashed down on him. Tucker disappeared.

Wipeout. No big deal for Tucker, though. He popped right up in the water and grabbed his board, which was tied to his ankle. He was all right. But the man on the raft wasn't. He thrashed around in the water screaming that he couldn't swim.

As that big black cloud spread across the sky toward them, the wind and waves grew rougher. Wanting to help the man, but concerned about his own safety, Tucker hesitated, then straddled his surfboard and, using his hands for oars, paddled toward the raft. He'd have time to get the guy's raft back to him and then head in. But as Tucker passed, the man lunged at the surfboard, knocking Tucker off.

And then this guy grabbed hold of Tucker! Wrapped up in that big bear's arms and legs, with the sea getting choppier, Tucker said he knew he was about to die. He began to pray.

But something lifted Tucker up through the water and onto his surfboard, where he was able to catch his breath. That's when he saw his friend Richard in the water, too! Have mercy! Richard was hauling that raft toward the man. With two big heaves, Richard snatched that guy straight up out of the water and onto the raft.

Richard yelled, "Let's push and pull it, Tugboat! Push and pull it in!"

Somehow Tucker and Richard pushed and pulled that raft—with the guy glued to it—close enough to shore that the man was able to wade in the rest of the way. Four or five people splashed into the water and helped them onto the beach and into the pier house. One of the helpers was a reporter on vacation.

As soon as everybody was inside the pier house, the rain poured down. An arrow of lightning whizzed across the pier into the water and lit up the whole ocean. That's when Tucker said he got scared, seeing that lightning. He'd have been fried alive, you know. The guy Tucker rescued was named Nibbles. Mr. Nibbles was so grateful that he gave Tucker a hundred dollars right on the spot.

The reporter interviewed everybody and took pictures of Tucker, Nibbles, and Tucker's dad, who almost had a heart attack when he heard what happened. When the reporter asked how such a small boy was able to rescue a big, grown man, Tucker said, "'Cause I'm a tugboat, like Richard said. We pull the big ones in."

But when Tucker turned around to point out Richard, he couldn't find him.

The reporter's story about Tucker's rescue was in the local paper, then got picked up by the Associated Press and went all over the world. CBS TV even flew him and his folks to New York to be on its morning show. Afterwards, back home in Morehead City, strangers stopped Tucker on the street, in stores, even came to his home. They wanted to see the little "tugboat" that hauled in that big man, and get his autograph.

Businesses up and down Arendell Street put up WELCOME HOME, TUGBOAT! posters in their windows. And there was a parade. Tucker was a hero! He and the mayor rode on the back of a big ole white Cadillac convertible and waved at everybody. I was so proud that I almost forgot and hollered out, "Way to go, Tootsie Roll!" but I caught myself in time.

Everybody—even local folks—called Tucker Tugboat after that, including us kids. We'd never seen a real live hero close up before, especially one our age. It wasn't cool anymore to tease him with those other names. Funny how things can turn right around, isn't it?

And you know what? Tucker grew to be six feet five. He played on the North Carolina Central University Eagles basketball team, joined the U.S. Coast Guard, and lives in Kill Devil Hills, North Carolina, on the Outer Banks.

But there's something Tucker never figured out. When

he first told people that Richard was the real hero, nobody believed him. Apparently nobody but Tucker had seen Richard—not even Mr. Nibbles.

There's more. When Tucker went into the pier gift shop to spend some of his rescue money, he picked up a book about the coast guard. He was thumbing through it when he stopped at an old-timey picture of some black men wearing jackets like Richard's. They were standing in front of a building on the Outer Banks. Below it was a picture of—yes, Richard! Mustache, beard, jacket, everything!

Tucker read, "History of the Pea Island Lifesaving Service. Captain Richard Etheridge was Keeper of the Pea Island Lifesaving Service, a forerunner of part of what is now the U.S. Coast Guard. This unique, all African American, courageous lifesaving crew, and those who followed, saved hundreds of shipwrecked passengers' lives by plunging into the stormy seas and bringing their charges back to safety."

Tucker said he shot out of that gift shop toward the restaurant to show his dad the book to prove his case, but what he read next made him stop: "Captain Etheridge, born in 1844 on Roanoke Island in North Carolina, died in 1900."

Tucker said he read that date fifteen or twenty times before it started to sink in. Nineteen hundred? Richard

Etheridge had been dead for almost one hundred years. How was it possible a dead man helped him save that guy? Unless Richard was a ghost. He'd been talking to, and swimming with—a ghost?

You can believe Tucker hit up the library that very next day and searched for as much information as he could find on Richard Etheridge. There wasn't much, but what he read was that Richard Etheridge was all those great things he had read about and that he still died in 1900.

A few years later, when Tucker's folks visited the North Carolina Aquarium on Roanoke Island, Tucker found Richard Etheridge's grave and monument. Etheridge's headstone was marked 1844–1900. That's when Tucker stopped talking about Richard being involved in the rescue. Unless somebody asked.

So now, if you run into Tucker "Tugboat" Willis, ask him about the rescue, and he'll tell you. Then, real carefully, ask if he ever met Richard Etheridge. He'll tell you yes, he did, and what he learned. What he learned was that it pays to be polite to everybody you meet, like Tucker was to a man named Richard. You never know when that person might help you.

And every time Tucker tells me the story, he tells it to me the same way I told it to you. Seeing how Tucker turned out proves that some mighty things that help folks out in some mighty big ways can come in some mighty small packages.

It also proves that good things come to those who wait, like I did. I know, because I'm Mrs. LaShana Mae Willis, Tugboat's wife.

There really was a man named Richard Etheridge, a professional fisherman who was born in 1842 on Roanoke Island off North Carolina. A member of the Thirty-sixth U.S. Colored Troops of the Union Army, he fought at the Battle of New Market Heights in Virginia during the Civil War. And in 1880, Etheridge was hired as the Keeper of the Pea Island Lifesaving Station on the Barrier Islands (the Outer Banks) of North Carolina. The station continued to set a high standard of performance with its all-Black personnel until 1947, when the Coast Guard closed down the facilities.

No one made any formal recognition of the Pea Island surfmen's daring sea rescues until 1996. In March of that year, Etheridge and his men were finally acknowledged posthumously in formal ceremonies in Washington, D.C., with a Gold Lifesaving Medal from the United States Coast Guard. Etheridge and his wife and daughter are buried on the grounds of the North Carolina Aquarium in Manteo, which maintains an exhibit on these brave men.

What Goes Around Comes Around

―◆―

"Taneshia, I want a boyfriend for Christmas," said Sudsey. "What do I do?"

"Boyfriend? I don't know," I said. I petted my cat, Rahima, who was lying on top of the couch behind me. "I thought we were supposed to be thinking of ways for me to not have to vacuum the downstairs carpet and wash the dishes."

"Come on now, Taneshia. You asked me for help getting out of housework. I'm trying to help you. Now you help me."

"All right, all right. Let me think." I started flipping through the TV channels with the remote control, but stopped when a lady came on the BET channel talking about how she could see into the future. "There you go," I said. "Call the psychic hotline."

"Call it for me." Sudsey grabbed my pen off the table and wrote the number on the palm of her hand. "You know Momma won't let me call nobody on TV anymore, not after we ordered those dolls from the Holiday Shopping Network last year."

We had bought two seventy-five-dollar Princess Ntombinde dolls with Sudsey's momma's American Express credit card. I didn't know somebody still had to pay real money to the credit card company. The company wouldn't take back the dolls because we cut off all their hair, so Momma had to reimburse Sudsey's momma. Then Momma made me pay *her* off by making me scrub and vacuum for a dollar a day. Seventy-five days! I've hated doing housework ever since.

This all happened about the same time Momma and Daddy got separated. Daddy lived in Saginaw, Michigan, which was a long, long, long way off from us. I missed him a lot. When he left, he gave me Rahima to remember him by. I wondered if calling this psychic hotline could help get Momma and Daddy back together again, too.

Sudsey nudged me with her socked toe. "I'll dare ya two bucks to call."

"Let me think," I said again. I loved to take Sudsey up on a dare, because I usually won. She wasn't as smart as me, even though she was twelve and in sixth grade. I was only ten. "Where're you gonna find a boy here in Morehead City, North Carolina, who's not kin to you? Sudsey, if I'm gonna call the psychic hotline you gotta dare me five dollars."

"Deal. Now call."

"What boy are you chasing so bad that you're gonna give up five dollars?"

"Roslyn says by sixth grade everybody should have had their first official kiss. I told her I'd had my first kiss, but I haven't."

"Why're you so worried about what Roslyn says?" I asked.

"'Cause I don't want her to find out the truth and tease me."

"That's stupid," I said, "and so is Roslyn." That was about the tenth time this afternoon that Sudsey had mentioned her name. Made me sick. I knew all about teasing, though. I was skinny, so sometimes kids call me Tree and Bones.

"You're on," I said, "but I'm only doing it 'cause we're best friends and you promised about my housework. Do the pledge." We stood up and bumped each other's right elbows together, then we turned and bumped each other's right hips, then we snapped our fingers three times and did one high five. That made it a deal, no backing down.

But when I called the hotline, I got put on hold. I hated to hold, so I hung up. Thank goodness this was a toll-free number, because I got put on hold ten times and never did get through.

"Now you gotta help me," I said. Sudsey told me to only vacuum the middle of the living room carpet, so that's all I did. Sudsey brought a dirty spaghetti plate over to Rahima's face. "Lick it," she said. But Rahima jumped off the couch and walked stiff-legged to the fireplace.

Sudsey stuck the dirty dishes under the sink. She even placed the stinky pot of navy beans that I'd scorched the other night down there. I reminded myself to take them all out and wash them after dinner tonight. Momma would never know.

I walked Sudsey back down the road to our meeting place by the old house. "Keep calling till you get through," Sudsey said. "When I get the boy, you get your money. This is the most important thing in my life." We said good-bye under the magnolia tree in the middle of the property. I hoped nobody ever bought that house because that spot was our meeting place.

Momma was home when I returned. She sat on the couch with her laptop computer beside her, looking over some papers. "Hey, big girl," she said. "How was school?"

I said, "Oh, same ole thing." I could see dust balls under the couch where the rug ended.

Momma glanced around the room and smiled a little. "Everything you do to help me make this place look decent is so good." But when she stood up and walked toward the kitchen, I about croaked. A million brown-and-white cat hairs floated off her skirt and followed her.

"Sudsey wants to get a boyfriend," I said as I set the table for dinner. "She says she can find out by calling that psychic hotline."

"I got some advice for her, and she doesn't need to call anywhere." Momma took hamburger patties and a package of frozen broccoli out of the refrigerator as she spoke. "Tell her to do her homework and leave the boys alone. Why does she need a boyfriend?" Momma stared hard at me behind her big round gold glasses and pretended to frown. "Hold up. Are you talking about Sudsey, or yourself? Boyfriend! You have a hard enough time taking care of Rahima. See how she's rubbing—here, stop! Cat hairs everywhere! Taneshia, have you brushed her lately?"

Momma opened cupboards and drawers, searching for her red-handled skillet. She found it, too. "Taneshia Ambrosia Butler, I'm not even going to ask how these dirty dishes got here," she said. "I'm going to pretend that I hear hot water running and that I see suds flying."

I hauled right on over to the sink, twisted on the hot water, and started washing quick.

When the telephone rang, Momma answered it. The

first thing out of her mouth was, "Taneshia just asked me how to get a boyfriend through that psychic hotline. I know. The things they put on TV just waiting for idle minds. For Sudsey, she said. I wasn't born yesterday. Here, Taneshia, it's Grankie."

Grankie was my grandmother Zanzibar Dorcas. Grankie was my name for her. She lived in a fancy double-wide trailer in Havelock over in the next county. After her daughters—my momma and my aunt Trippy—got grown, Grankie became an actress and traveled around the world with the Afrika Strutters Theater until Momma and Daddy got separated. Then she retired and came back home to us.

Thanks to Momma, Grankie drilled me for three whole minutes about whether I had a boyfriend. "I'm just checking," she said. "I need to know, in case you're planning to get married anytime soon, so I can get my dress ready."

I liked talking to my grandmother. She could always make me feel warm inside. "No, Grankie, no."

That night in bed, as I listened to my favorite singer, Tevin Campbell, on my CD player, I thought about Sudsey wanting a boyfriend. I began to think about who I would want for a boyfriend. You know, just for make-believe. I fell asleep with Tevin singing his heart out, just for me.

Three days after that, just before Thanksgiving, Rahima and I were sitting on the couch doing my homework. I saw a letter propped up against the lamp on the cocktail table. It was addressed to me. Since I don't get much mail except from my dad, I tore open that envelope fast. Inside was a flier: "Want to get the guy of your dreams? Mother Gratify can help you. No age restrictions. Call between the hours of 3 P.M. and 5 P.M. Pacific standard time. No charge to calling party."

I couldn't believe my eyes! No charge! I almost squashed Rahima stretching for the telephone. At first I was going to call Sudsey. But I decided to call this Mother Gratify first, just to check her out. I tried to figure out what "Pacific standard time" meant, but finally I gave up and dialed.

"Hello, I want to speak to Mother Gratify about getting a boyfriend," I said.

"Who's this?"

"It's me, Taneshia, Mrs. Mother Gratify. You sent me this flier, remember?"

"Oh, oh yes, of course. Just one moment."

By now my heart was pounding like a drum. I told myself to also ask about whether I'd get a computer for Christmas. And if my folks would get back together again.

A woman with a Spanish accent said hello. "I am Mother Gratify. And you are Taneshia Butler, of course."

"How'd you know my last name?"

"I say what I see," she said.

"Wow. I'm calling for my friend. She wants a boyfriend for Christmas."

"Uh-*hunh*. But didn't that flier tell you to call me between three and five P.M. Pacific standard time?"

"I—yeah, but I didn't know what time that was."

"It won't be possible for you to get your friend's wish fulfilled if you can't follow my directions. Anyway, how old is Sudsey?"

"Twelve—hey, how'd you know her name?"

"Because I say what I see. Isn't Sudsey kind of young for a boyfriend?"

"I don't know. Miz Gratify, are you sure this isn't going to cost me anything?"

"Not all things are paid for with money. Or credit cards. However, you happened to be the one thousandth person from Morehead City to send up a wish for a boyfriend, so you get three free calls. This is number one. What do you think of that?"

"I don't know, 'cause I never won anything before." I decided to test her. "Can you tell my horoscope? Do I get a birthday reading? Do you use tarot cards? How'd you know what my address was? Do you know my mother or grandmother?"

"So many questions. How can you listen? And if you don't want to listen, you can always hang up so that someone else can call me."

"I'm sorry," I said. But Mother Gratify didn't really seem mad. I decided I liked the sound of her voice. It sounded like how warm gingerbread would if it could make a noise—spicy.

"You're forgiven," said Mother Gratify. "Now tell me what kind of boyfriend Sudsey wants."

"One with lots of money and who drives a red convertible. She wants him to take her to—uh, Busch Gardens in Virginia, and to Mexico and Bermuda, take her jet skiing—"

"Child, she doesn't need to have a boyfriend to do that," said Mother Gratify. "She just needs money. Tell her to work hard, maybe get a little after-school job, save up her money. Then maybe she and her momma and daddy and everybody can go somewhere next summer."

"But she can't wait that long. She needs him to be here by Christmas, in time to kiss her on New Year's Eve. And he can't have big feet." This wasn't going good at all.

"So she needs a rush job. All right. I see a good-looking young man, smart, mannerly, with black hair and deep brown eyes, smooth skin, somebody like, um . . . who's your favorite singer, Taneshia?"

"Tevin Campbell."

"Perhaps he looks like this Tevin Campbell."

"Ohh yes!" I blinked into the telephone's earpiece to see if I saw an eyeball looking back at me. Because Mother Gratify was looking right into my mind. Wait a minute! Did I really want Sudsey's boyfriend to look like Tevin Campbell?

"Miz Mother Gratify, could you, uh, save this one for—"

"Now, Taneshia, there's a procedure to getting a fellow through Mother Gratify."

My shoulders drooped. I should have known we'd have to pay, no matter what she said. "Well, maybe Sudsey can borrow her—"

"No, Sudsey doesn't need to borrow anything. I told you that payment is not always in money. You must listen to Mother Gratify and follow her directions exactly. So get a pencil, write this all down. Number one: Sudsey must clean her room ceiling to floor, wash her curtains, pick up every scrap of paper lying anywhere, vacuum or sweep under her bed, and clean out her closet."

"Wait, wait, wait. I'm trying to write this all down. Why's she gotta do all that? Is her boyfriend gonna be in

her room?" When Mother Gratify remained silent, I figured I better shut up and just write.

"All right. Number two: She must sweep or vacuum
the living room and the dining room, wash the dishes,
scrub and wax the kitchen floor. Number three: She
must dig the dirt out of the kitchen corners, and wipe
out the refrigerator each time anybody spills something
in it. That way her boyfriend will visit a tidy house where
he can sit down. She can offer him some juice or something in a clean glass. Because I understand that Sudsey
has twin three-year-old brothers who like to dirty up
stuff."

"You know everything. But this's a lot of work," I said.
I sure was glad I didn't have to do it. For a computer I'd
do it, but a boyfriend? Naw.

"Now, last. She must dust and sweep and keep her
room up every day. And scrub the kitchen floor once a
week."

The bump on my finger hurt from so much writing.
"Sudsey's gonna croak when she hears about this list," I
said, grinning. "I'm glad I only want a computer. Anything else?"

"Well, since you initiated this call, and if you want this
to work for Sudsey, you have to do the same things."

"Do what same things?"

"Everything you wrote down for Sudsey to do."

"That's not fair!"

"It's the only way Sudsey'll get that boyfriend. Doesn't she help you when you need help? What goes around comes around, you know. And if you do bad to her, it might come back on you. So you and Sudsey decide. You call me back at exactly one P.M. Pacific standard time next Tuesday, one week from today."

"But I can't do all this work!"

"And tell Sudsey to not let you snap at Mother Gratify anymore, either. Good-bye."

I hung up and slumped back on the couch. That lady's words scorched my eardrums so bad they made my face twist up tighter than the rubber bands around my braids. I punched the couch pillow hard, and Rahima sprang off the couch in a cloud of cat hairs. I dialed Sudsey's telephone number. This darn dare was off!

Binky and Buster, Sudsey's twin brothers, answered. "Sing it first," they said. They wouldn't turn the phone over to Sudsey until I sang the Barney song to them.

"So Sudsey, you better bring your fat legs over here and do all my work, too," I said after I snapped off the work list and Mother Gratify's warning to her.

"I need that boyfriend bad," said Sudsey. "Roslyn's having a Christmas party and she's only inviting couples."

"So?" I frowned. "If you get a boyfriend you can go, but I can't."

"Anyway, did you ask Mother Gratify what he looked like?"

"Tevin Campbell" slipped out before I could stop my lips.

Sudsey started to scream. "Shoot yes, I'll clean up my house for *him*! Tevin Campbell is fine! See, you got it made. You won't have anybody to clean up after now but you and your momma. I got Momma, Daddy, my dirt-head brothers, Uncle Simon, and me. Momma likes the boys better than me, so she makes me do all the work. C'mon, you promised. I need this boyfriend double bad!"

"Then have Roslyn call Mother Gratify for you."

"Hold up, Taneshia, hold up. Why you have to act like this? You got an attitude. Unless you really *do* want me to have Roslyn call Mother Gratify. I mean, if *you* really don't want to anymore." She let that hang in the air while I thought it over. "And I won't protect you next time Venita tries to pull your nose off through the back of your head."

"All right, all right, I'll do it. But you got me in a knot, Sudsey."

"Thanks, girlfriend. I knew you would. What makes you think I want Roslyn for my best friend? Her breath smells like a garbage dump."

After we finished talking, I picked up Rahima. "Seems like I'm getting the worst end of this deal, girl." Rahima purred and pressed her nose a little against my shoulder, like she understood.

For the next two hours I was washing dishes, sweeping the kitchen floor, and even stabbing the kitchen corners with the butter knife to pry out the crud I had let pile up from previous moppings. Then I squirted out the whole bottle of cleaning stuff and waxed the floor.

By the time I finished, my hands were puffy with water blisters, and my back ached. But the kitchen was sparkling clean. I don't think I'd ever cleaned it this thoroughly before. I don't think Momma had either, not even when Daddy was still here.

When Momma got home, she strolled into the kitchen and—*swoosh!*—slid across the slick floor, bumped into me, and ended up squashed against me and the refrigerator.

"I waxed the floor," I said as she and I untangled.

"No kidding," she said. "Mercy! Talk about being knocked off my feet." She looked around. "Taneshia, I don't know what's got into you, but I sure do love it. Thank you, baby. The kitchen looks so clean, we ought to celebrate. Let's go to McDonald's, hunh?"

"Sure!" We hadn't done that in ages.

The next afternoon after school, I vacuumed most of Rahima's hairs from the couch. I even dusted. When I telephoned Sudsey, she wasn't there, so I went to work on my homework. When Momma came home from work, she was so pleased she was grinning from braid to braid. She said, "You've turned into the Energizer bunny, Taneshia. You're making things easier for me around here, honey, and I really appreciate it. I know it's been rough with your father not here, but it's been rough for me, too."

She slipped her arm around my shoulders. "You deserve a break, and I do, too. How about a movie?"

"All right!" I hadn't thought much about what it was like for her without Daddy. They had argued a lot at the end. It was nice to make Momma so happy.

The next morning was Thanksgiving. Momma and I fixed breakfast. While we ate in her bed, we watched the Macy's parade on TV. Then we drove over to Grankie's for dinner. We all ate so much that the buttons on our clothes almost popped off. Afterwards I lay on the couch watching Grankie's video of Eddie Murphy in *The Nutty Professor* while Momma and Grankie played a card game called bid whist with Uncle Reggie and Aunt Trippy.

Grankie popped down the ace of spades on Uncle Reggie's king and made him and Aunt Trippy lose that hand. "Taneshia, do you know what you want for Christmas?" Aunt Trippy asked.

"A Hewlett-Packard Pavilion computer with CD-ROM

drive and high-resolution graphics and e-mail and a fax, all the games, I want to get on the Internet and have—"

"Listen to this child. This child knows exactly what she wants. Good luck!" Aunt Trippy said. "And how's your girlfriend, Sudsey?"

"She's fine."

"With Sudsey in middle school," Aunt Trippy went on, "isn't she kind of old for you to hang around with? You know what they say: 'Tell me who you hang out with and I'll tell you who you are.'"

"She's only twelve," I said, glancing at Momma.

"Sudsey's all right, Trippy," said Momma. "With Taneshia not having an older sister, Sudsey's a big help. Like how we were."

"Yeah, well, VaLesta, maybe if you and Truman had stayed together, Taneshia could be a big sister to her own little sisters or brothers," Aunt Trippy told Momma. She was so nosy.

"Well, if you hadn't had your kids so soon, Taneshia'd have some cousins her own age now," Momma replied.

Everybody went, "Uh-oh, look out," and "Don't go there, VaLesta!" because Aunt Trippy was only nineteen when she had her first child.

Aunt Trippy just laughed. "But I bet what I told you isn't what Sudsey's telling Taneshia."

"Thank goodness," said Grankie, "because half the time what you told VaLesta didn't make any sense. Taneshia, you help Sudsey, Sudsey helps you. Do good, though. Don't do anything bad. What goes around comes around."

"I heard somebody else say that," I told Grankie.

"Who?" she asked. But I just smiled at my secret.

By next Tuesday, Sudsey and I were ready for our second set of instructions. And we were more than ready to dump all that cleaning. We met at my house to call Mother Gratify at four P.M., after Sudsey figured out the correct time.

"Ask her how old he is, where he lives, and what size are his shoes," Sudsey said. She checked her list of questions. "What sports does he like? What's his favorite food, so I can have it in our sparkling clean fridge when he comes over."

Mother Gratify answered on the first ring. I got that warm gingerbread feeling inside, like I did the first time.

"Let me talk to her," Sudsey yelled.

"No," said Mother Gratify, who must have heard Sudsey. "I can only talk to the person who initiated the call."

"Tell her I did everything you said she said to do," Sudsey ordered. "Ask her what I gotta do next."

"Now we move up to level two," said Mother Gratify.

"By the way, ask Sudsey how she feels helping around the house."

When I asked, Sudsey answered, "Tell her I love it," with a wink, but I shook my head no.

Mother Gratify asked how my mother liked my cleaning. "She was happy, 'cause I didn't do it very well before. After Daddy left—they're separated—I didn't want to do it at all. I wanted to ask you—" Sudsey nudged me and jerked her thumb at herself. "Okay, okay, Sudsey wants to know what else she's got to do."

"All right. A boy likes a smart young lady. How are Sudsey's grades?"

I covered the mouthpiece of the telephone. "Bad news. She said boys like smart girls."

"I'm smart. Smart enough. You're the one who can't do fractions. Tell her I get all As."

"I'll accept that," Mother Gratify said when I told her, "even though I'm receiving negative vibrations as to the validity of that response. Next, we must discuss the Courtesy Factor. A boyfriend appreciates a young lady who has good manners. He must have good manners, too, of course. Does Sudsey say 'thank you,' 'excuse me,' and 'please'? Does she take baths or showers every day, clean out the tub afterwards, use deodorant, brush her teeth, floss, and so on?"

"Sure," I said. I knew where this was headed. I hated to clean the tub. "Does this mean that—"

"For the next three weeks, until the Tuesday before Christmas, every time Sudsey says something she must say 'please' or 'thank you' or 'excuse me,' whatever's appropriate. That means you do, too, Taneshia."

"But we're through with all that cleaning, right?" I said.

"Wrong. You got to keep that up. Call me at this time three weeks from today. That'll be your last call."

"But—"

"I got to say what I see, Taneshia, and I see that young ladies who know how to be tidy, do their homework, make at least Cs, and have good manners get boyfriends like Tevin Campbell. Or a good substitute."

"But—" I stamped my foot.

"Now you tell me good-bye the way a young lady with good manners does."

"Good-bye, Miz Mother Gratify," I said real low.

I hung up and put my hands on my hips. "Sudsey, this is a nightmare. For the next three weeks, we got to say 'thank you' and 'yes ma'am' and 'no ma'am,' 'please,' 'excuse me,' and all that every time we open our mouths. That's the Courtesy Factor. Plus the housework!"

Sudsey sighed. "This is harder than I thought."

"So are you ready to quit?"

"Nunh-uh. I told everybody at school I had a personal psychic who was getting me a boyfriend like Tevin Campbell," said Sudsey.

"But what if it doesn't happen? What if this is just some lady making it up?"

"Then it'll be your fault 'cause you're the one who called her," Sudsey said.

After another week I was ready to drop. I had just enough time after getting home from school to straighten up, do homework, eat and talk to Momma, take a bath, clean out the tub, and fall into bed with Rahima. But seeing Momma smile at me more made me happier, too. We ate out twice that week, and went Christmas shopping that Friday. I didn't see Sudsey much. When I called her on the telephone, she only had a few minutes to talk, or she wasn't there. I wondered if she was running around with that Roslyn.

I had another big problem, too, now—fractions. I was getting Ds and Mother Gratify said I had to get Cs. When Daddy made his weekly call that night, was I ever glad to hear his voice. I was ready to bawl over those dumb fractions. When I told him I was going batty over math, we went right to work, right over the telephone. Mom let me use her computer. I e-mailed the word problems to him, and he rewrote them and e-mailed them back. I was able to figure out the answers a lot quicker that way.

I must have written 'please' and 'thank you' to him a million times, and said them to Momma, too. They were both so surprised that all Dad could do was write back, "Well, thank you, too!" And Momma would smile. It was almost like old times, with Momma and me and Dad working together, even if he was in Michigan and it was just word problems and fractions.

I asked Daddy if he was coming home for Christmas. "It depends on what Momma says," he wrote.

"We'll discuss it," was all she said.

Finally, the Tuesday before Christmas arrived. The clock on the stove said five till four. Sudsey didn't show up until nearly four-thirty. "Where've you been?" I said, opening the door. "Mother Gratify's gonna be mad at us for not following directions. I thought you'd be here earlier."

Sudsey dragged me outside and pointed to a beat-up red Ford Escort with blue smoke puffing out the back in my front yard. A long-necked boy with braids was at the wheel. Beside him sat a girl I recognized as Roslyn. A couple of kids were in the backseat.

"So?" I said, pulling back when I saw Roslyn.

"It's *him*! My boyfriend!" Sudsey whispered out a scream. "I mean, almost. He's Roslyn's cousin from Raleigh. He and his folks are down for Christmas. My wish came true! Well, not yet, but I'm working on it. He's sixteen! Were you really doing all that housework? I didn't have time to, so I paid Binky and Buster to help. Tell Mother Gratify thanks. Bye!" Sudsey flew across the yard and got into the car.

Shocked, I opened my mouth to tell her "Wait!" But I shut it as I watched the car leave. The chilly December wind hit me. I hurried back inside and slumped on the couch. Rahima looked up at me with her little heart-shaped face like she felt sorry for me. I petted her and fought off tears. I felt like an old tin can out rusting in the woods, used up, empty, thrown out.

Sudsey got her wish, and she was running with Roslyn. I didn't even get my five dollars. So much for best friends and promises. I decided to call Mother Gratify anyway. But I was sure it was too late for her to help me with my wishes.

When I explained why I was calling so late, Mother Gratify didn't sound upset. "My dear, I'm glad Sudsey got what she wanted. That was the purpose of you calling in the first place, wasn't it, for your friend?"

"Yeah. But Mother Gratify, Sudsey's hanging around another girl now, and I guess maybe they're gonna be best friends, even though I did help her out," I said in a rush. "And now she's gone and I don't have a best friend anymore."

"Sometimes even best friends do stupid things. She's

still your best friend. Sudsey won't last very long around Roslyn, I bet. That boy won't want Sudsey, either. He'll think she's a child. Which she is. Is there anything else you want to ask me?"

"Well. I don't know if you can help me with this, but here goes." I told her how I wished my folks could get back together.

"Mm-hmm. I know that's been bothering you. It'll take a lot more than you doing housework to get them back together, though," said Mother Gratify. "Remember that it's not your fault they're apart. Your momma and daddy's gonna have to work it out. You just keep on being there for them, and they'll be there for you, separate or together. Things work out the best way they can. I bet your daddy sees you at Christmas. You're such a sweet child. Mother Gratify just loves you. And your grandmother loves you, too. In fact, I suggest that you look out your window right now. You might be surprised by what you see."

I pulled open the kitchen curtains and peered outside. I saw Grankie's silver Town Car parked outside our house. Up the road, I saw a long U-Haul truck parked at the old house.

"Mother Gratify, excuse me, I got to go. My Grankie's—I mean my grandmother's outside, please," I said as politely as I could. "Thank you for your advice. I'm glad I got to talk with you. You know what? You're just like my Grankie."

"That's because I *am* your Grankie. Come on out to the car."

"What?" I hung up the telephone and ran outside.

"Grankie?" I said. "Were you—"

"Technology's a wonderful thing, isn't it?" said Grankie in a voice that sounded just like Mother Gratify. She held up her cellular phone.

"So that's how Mother Gratify knew everything! Grankie, you're something else! I guess only somebody who knows me real good would know how to help, hunh? You're the best psychic anybody could have."

Before I could say anything else, she pointed to a boy about my age walking toward us. He looked just like Tevin Campbell. Or maybe like his younger brother. Sort of. He came over to Grankie's side of the car. "Excuse me, lady, we just moved into that house"—he pointed to the old house with the magnolia tree—"and we need to get our electricity turned on. Can my mom use your phone?"

That boy was talking to Grankie, but you know what? He was smiling right at me.

Slow and Steady Wins the Race

—————◆—————

Dipping his green head beneath the water, Mudslider paddled cautiously toward the source of the ripples in the Pond. Ripples like this meant that the human was throwing food into the water again. If he hurried, he would find food floating in the water or drifting down onto the Pond's muddy floor. Unless, of course, the other, bigger snapping turtles, the grackles, the blue jays, and the crows got to it again before he did. He opened his little beak and snapped at a tadpole going by. Maybe today would be different.

Mudslider rose to the surface and lifted his small snapping turtle head above the water. For a few seconds, he rested his legs. It was a quiet, warm July morning. That awful Pond Poisoning he had last spring still made him weak. The poisoning came from low-lying, nasty-smelling clouds that settled upon the Pond each spring. The clouds were supposed to kill mosquito larvae, which the young turtles and other animals loved to eat. The older animals and birds had learned not to eat the larvae when the clouds came. No one, however, had ever warned the younger ones about it.

When Mudslider noticed four other young snapping turtles moving forward, he started off, too. "Take your time," he heard one of them say to the others. "We don't have to worry about ole Mudslider getting to the food first."

"I'm doing all right," Mudslider said, and snapped at them to remind them that his jaws could bite just as good as theirs. Come on, legs, he told himself firmly. Swim, swim, swim! Stir those stumps!

He paused when he saw Great Gran Snappy, the Pond's ruling elder and the granddaddy of all the snapping turtles. All the Pond folks said the old snapping turtle was "the biggest, the baddest, the boldest, the oldest, the meanest, the fightingest, *and* the greediest snapping turtle the world has ever known." Great Gran Snappy lay at the bottom of the Pond under some logs, looking like a moss-covered slab of rock half buried in the mud. But Mudslider knew that Gran Snappy didn't miss a thing through those half-closed piercing yellow-and-black eyes. Unsuspecting tadpoles, crayfish, whirli-gig beetles, water striders, snakes, and even a couple of young loons who wandered past that "rock" got caught and eaten regularly. Gran Snappy liked to say, "Every shut eye ain't 'sleep."

Rumor had it that Gran Snappy even ate his own grandkids from time to time. So whenever Mudslider stopped by to pay his respects, he did it from a distance.

Not far from Gran Snappy was another big snapper called Ripper, the next heir to the Pond. Or at least he acted like he was. Ripper dangled in the water close to the shore with only his wrinkled green head showing. When several pieces of food hit the water, Ripper's head disappeared. He and the other larger snappers swarmed around the food, snapping at each other's long tails and jaws as much as at the food.

Mudslider swam in a wide circle around the feeders, searching for something to eat. Just then a tan spongy blob smacked the water, and Mudslider turned toward it.

"Move it, mud worm!" a hefty pond slider turtle yelled as it churned toward the food. Mudslider swerved away. But instinct and his growling stomach sent him right back to the fringes of the feeding circle. There! There! A tiny fragment swollen with water floated by. Mudslider shot out his neck and gulped down the thick pasty dough. Pizza crust!

Another wedge of crust, almost the size of Mudslider, hit the water nearby. Mudslider snapped at it, grabbed it, and eagerly pulled it to himself. He stuffed as much of it into his mouth as he could, amazed at his catch. But Ripper also spied the crust and barrelled toward Mudslider like a bowling ball. Mudslider paddled off as fast as his weak little legs could go. The pizza crust trailed behind him. Mudslider hid among the submerged branches of a downed oak tree, with the crust sticking out of his beak. Ripper's powerful hooked jaws slashed at the crust, missed, and instead fastened on to a small oak branch. He snapped it in half, nipping at Mudslider's cheek as he went by. Abandoning the crust, Mudslider sucked his head and legs and tail inside his shell as Ripper spun around for another attack.

"Leave the boy alone!" someone hissed.

Ripper hesitated at the command. Then, snatching the crust and churning up mud in Mudslider's face, the big snapping turtle swam away.

Mudslider huddled in his shell, his cheek stinging. "At least you still have your head," he told himself. And somebody scared Ripper off, but who? Just once Mudslider wished that he could stand his ground and fight back.

When he thought it was safe, Mudslider pushed his head out and looked around for Ripper. He also looked around for the other snappers, the white heron, the raccoon, and the muskrat, who tried to eat him from time to time, too. Then he began another search for food among the bladderwort branches spreading out across the water. He was so hungry he would have even eaten gnats. Finally he spied a sliver of crust that the human had thrown floating by the stems of some water hyacinths. But before he could get to it, a little bluegill darted over, gobbled it up, and sped off.

"Here! That's mine!" Mudslider paddled after the fish for a few feet until a water spider strode by. Mudslider snapped at it and missed. Finally he straggled over to the side of a log to catch his breath. He nibbled at the bark. Shoot. He'd never get big and strong this way.

"You 'bout lost your head over that piece of bread," said someone right over him.

With a start Mudslider stared up into the frowning face of Great Gran Snappy, who sat on top of the log, right above his head. Gran Snappy lowered his big bald wrinkled head, stretched his long thick neck, and opened his beaked, cavernous mouth inches from Mudslider's nose. Mudslider hissed, pushed backward from the fearsome green-black jaws and tried to cover himself up in the mud.

"Excuse me for yawning in your face," Gran Snappy said. "Sun makes me sleepy. Well, there you go. That Old Gal comes out here throwing hamburger buns and pizza crust and wieners and chicken skins and whatnot in the water. You all get to squabbling over it worse than a flock of ducks after a corncob. Every summer I find one of you dead, floating by the cattails, bottom shell up, swollen, mouth open—if there's a head still there for a mouth to be open on. Relax, kid, and come on out where I can see you. Ain't enough of you there for me to bother trying to swallow you down. If I hadn't hollered at Ripper he woulda turned you into a yo-yo over that crust. Crusts and bread are no good for you. It turns into stuff that stops you up inside."

"Oh, I see," Mudslider said from inside his shell. "Thanks for stopping Ripper, Granddaddy. But that piece was the biggest one I ever had, until Ripper—"

"Yeah, yeah, but Ripper'll eat anything. He'd take a bite out of lightning if he could get to it. He's had Pond Poisoning twice. He doesn't have good sense. You're the one they call Mudslider, aren't ya? You're a snapping turtle, not a mud turtle. What was the name on your egg when you hatched out?"

"No one ever told me." Mudslider stayed in his shell. "Everybody's always called me Mudslider 'cause I still can't climb good from the Pond Poisoning I had last year. I'm always sliding back in the mud with the mud turtles. I'd get stronger if somebody wasn't always stealing my food. I wish I was like you. I bet you always get what you want."

"Well, kid, you got to know when to fight and when to flee. You sure won't see me fighting anybody over a chunk of bread. But you let that Old Gal throw out some fish guts and chicken skins and yeah, I'll fight for that. That's natural food. Chicken skin's hard to swallow, but it's some good eating. But for the best eating, give me a pear. Cleans you out, makes you strong."

"What's a pear?"

"Instinct and a growling stomach not told you about pears? You ain't ate honest-to-goodness turtle food if you ain't ate a pear. Wait here." Gran Snappy slid off the log. He swam to the edge of the pond, pulled his heavy girth onto the bank, and disappeared behind the rambling rose brambles. Mudslider stretched out his head to watch. Land! He'd heard too many turtle horror stories about its dangers to ever try to go. Gran Snappy must rule land by now, too.

In a few minutes Gran Snappy clumped back and slid into the water with an oval-shaped, green thing sticking out of his mouth. He swam toward Mudslider, who promptly pulled in his head. Gran Snappy dropped the pear on the Pond bottom and chomped into it.

"This," Gran Snappy said between bites, "is a pear. Good stuff. It's fruit. Natural. Here. Have some."

"Promise you won't eat me while I'm eating it?" Mudslider asked. Gran Snappy just blinked. With his head still shrunk back in his shell and watching Gran Snappy, Mudslider moved over to the pear pieces and nibbled on one. His jaws sprang open and closed over one chunk, then another. "Ummm! Granddaddy, this—this is good, it's—"

"Shut up and eat."

Mudslider bolted down the mushy, grainy morsels while Gran Snappy climbed back up on his log and watched him. "Good, hunh? We eat these from that tree that Old Gal planted next to the Pond for us. Nobody but me is still around who ever ate pears from her Great Golden Pear Tree that used to be yonderways by her nest. Those were *good* pears. I survived the most terrifyingest, wettest, windiest, longest journey a snapping turtle ever made because of those pears. Bring your young knock-kneed behind up here by me and I'll tell you what happened. C'mere. C'mon. Now!"

"Oh boy," Mudslider muttered to himself. "Come on, legs." He scrabbled at the wet, slippery log with his tiny claws and got nowhere. When Gran Snappy opened his big beak and leaned toward him, Mudslider hissed, "Don't eat me!" Gran Snappy, however, slid his mouth over both of Mudslider's front legs and pulled him onto the log.

From his new seat, Mudslider could see the pear tree by the Pond, the tops of the weeping willow stumps poking out of the water, all of the Pond, and in the distance, a huge square object that looked like a giant rock, a million times bigger than even Gran Snappy. "Oh man, you can see everything from here," he whispered.

"Kid, you ain't seen nothing yet. Now sit still and listen," Gran Snappy said. "Back in the old days, you weren't considered to be a grown snapping turtle until you went out into the world and carried back a Great Golden Pear and gave it to Cruncher. Cruncher ruled the turtles then. I was young and dumb—about like you, but bigger—when I went. But my trip was special. I went to save Cruncher's life."

"How?"

"Cruncher craved those Great Golden Pears, so it was a high honor for us to go out and bring him back some. It took two sunlights and two nighttimes to make the trip, and one out of three snappers who left never came back."

"Because they had weak legs like mine?" Mudslider asked.

"No, no. Snapping turtles were some fearsome folks then. Jaws like clams, shells harder than rocks, big as boulders. Cruncher must have weighed fifty pounds himself. Nobody but humans, alligators, and raccoons messed with those guys. Humans, you see, loved snapping turtle stew. Raccoons and alligators, well, you know about them.

"Anyway, that summer Cruncher got sick with Pond Poisoning. The only thing he said would make him well was to eat pears from the Great Golden Pear Tree. Me and two other snappers, Yellow Shell and Scaler, stepped up to go get them. When dusk fell, we three left the Pond, not knowing if we'd ever return. Yellow Shell headed up the embankment to the left. Scaler went straight ahead into the wild rose brambles. I set out to the right for the creek bed that eventually curved over toward Old Gal's nest. That's that big square rock you see. Cruncher said there'd be water in the creek, and food. But, shoot, when I reached the creek, it was as dry as a shriveled-up leaf. It did offer a hiding place, so I went along that creek bed all night, took a short rest, woke up, and struck out again.

"When the sunlight came in, it brought with it a layer of clouds and a burning, wet, salty breeze. Which felt good to me. But as the day went on, it began to rain. The wind picked up. It picked up some more, then it began to blow so hard it blew the rain sideways instead of up and down. It bent the trees first one way then the other, broke off branches, tossed them up in the air, then smashed them to the ground. It pushed trees over and made their roots stick up to the sky.

"I took all this into account as I walked along, you know. It occurred to me that that wind could toss me up in the air, too, and flip me over on my back. A turtle's nightmare! Turkey buzzards and crows would be on me pecking out my eyes and my tongue, eating me piece by piece right out of my shell if I ended up like that. So I packed my head back in my shell. I walked real careful, real slow, steady, one foot, and the other and the other and the other, digging each claw right down into the mud to keep hold to the ground.

"That day I also learned to never trust a dry creek. One second I was walking in the mud, and the next here came a wall of water and I was fighting to swim against the current. I went under twice. The third time I broke the surface and what did I see? A great big tree limb headed straight for me! Just before it rammed into my head, I clawed my way out of that water and up the side of the creek bank. I clung to a thick patch of kudzu vines anchored to the trunk of a cedar tree. Why, if that big branch had hit me, it would have dragged me clear down to the alligator swamp, and they'd have gotten me instead of the turkey buzzards. For the rest of the night, that's where I stayed, in those vines.

"The next morning the sky was clear and the air was hot. The storm was gone. When I looked around, all I saw were uprooted and broken trees and limbs. And finally I saw what I'd set out for—the Great Pear Tree. I recognized it from Cruncher's description. But the tree had toppled over onto the Old Gal's nest. Cruncher's precious Golden Pears were scattered and squashed on the ground.

"The worst was yet to come, though. I knew I had to reach those pears before they turned rotten and before the deerflies, black birds, rabbits, deer, and worse yet, the raccoons, got to them. A raccoon'll drive a snapping turtle crazy, with those little paws picking and poking at you and whatnot.

"You know that being fast in the water is easy for, well, most turtles. But being fast on land is like saying we can fly. And that's when I started to get a little worried, because I was going to have to climb fast over, under, and through those fallen tree branches to reach those pears in time. It'd take too long to go around them. I sat there and thought about it a little. Finally I decided that, by golly, I'd come this far and I was gonna eat me a pear from the Great Pear Tree, no matter what. At first I was gonna do it for Cruncher, but then I decided that I was gonna do it for myself, to prove I was grown.

"So I struck out. You never saw such a careful climbing, pulling, pushing, biting, twisting, jerking, snapping, moving-fast-as-he-could-go snapping turtle in your life. I got through it. The rabbits and the raccoons were already chomping when I appeared. I was covered with wet leaves and mud, and pieces of kudzu vine, but I didn't care. The other animals stopped and watched me march by. They'd probably never seen a snapping turtle climb trees before. I headed straight to a pear tree branch on the ground, plopped myself down on one end, opened my jaws just as wide as I could, claimed that limb as mine, and dared anybody to mess with me. They didn't.

"I sniffed a pear, and then I bit into it. Never had I ever tasted anything as sweet, as juicy, as perfect as that pear. I was starving, and I ate and ate until I was about to bust out my shell. Slow and steady, I done what I said I was gonna do. I got those pears. And now I was grown for sure. I stayed right where I was, and that's where I went to sleep.

"When I woke up I had to battle the deerflies plastered on my face, sucking on the pear juice. I just ate 'em, and that ended that. Now all I had to do was get back. Just about dark, I dined on some more of those glorious pears, and then I prepared to leave. I snapped off a small limb near me with several pears hanging from the top branches. I could drag that limb with those pears safe at the top right on back home. So I did.

"I jerked that limb awhile, then I pulled it awhile, taking my time, watching out, feet firm to the ground for holding power. I had that branch so tight in my mouth, why, nothing could have pulled it loose.

"I was almost to the creek bed, fixing to follow it back on land, when I heard a pop, and something like lightning burrowed into my right shoulder. It was like the worst thorn you could ever have stick into you. Two humans appeared. Apparently they planned to have me for their snapping turtle stew. They banged around in the brush looking for me, but I stayed still. Finally they left. I passed out with my branch still tight in my mouth.

"When I came to, I was being lifted into the air. It was Old Gal had me in her paws. I couldn't run, but I wasn't going to let her make me into stew, either, not without a fight. 'Cause sometimes you have to take a stand. So I let go of my branch. I snapped at her, clawed at her, I even beat at her with my tail. She wouldn't turn me loose. She carried me into her nest. She covered my head with something so I couldn't bite her. And then, you know what?"

"What?" cried Mudslider with his mouth open. "She ate you?"

"Now if she'd done that, I wouldn't be here to tell the tale, would I? No, she made the pain in my shoulder go away. I had been shot by a smooth, shiny, red, round pebble harder than a rock. She took it out of my shoulder. For the next several sunlights and nighttimes, she fed me those wonderful Golden Pears and worked on my shoulder until I got better," Gran Snappy said. "When I was able to move again she carried me back to the Pond."

"Oh, Granddaddy, you're so brave," Mudslider breathed. "Touched and attacked by humans and pebbles and still lived to tell the tale. But wasn't Cruncher angry that you didn't bring back any pears?"

"Oh, this is the best part," Gran Snappy said. When Old Gal brought Gran Snappy back, she also left a bunch of Golden Pears with him. Cruncher came up first and ate. With the Pond so full of tree branches, it was hard for most of the big snappers to get around for food, so Cruncher let any other turtle who wanted one eat, too. Yellow Shell and Scaler were there. They had turned back as soon as the rain began. Afterwards, Old Gal planted the pear tree by the Pond so the turtles wouldn't have to go out into the world again to find food. "But these pears aren't as sweet as those first ones," said Gran Snappy.

Mudslider just stared at Gran Snappy. Would he ever have the courage and the strength to walk on land to get a pear? "These sure taste good to me," Mudslider said.

"No comparison, kid. These taste like the Pond with a north wind on a cloudy day. A Great Golden Pear tastes like clear water after a storm, with blue sky and a hot sun. They're probably what made me live so long, and made me so wise, and so big. I don't even know if the Great Golden Pear Tree by Old Gal's nest survived or not. Nobody's ever gone back to check. But before I die, I wish I could have just one more Golden Pear off it. Why, if I was dying again and ate one of those Golden Pears, I bet I'd come back to the land of the live, just like I did before."

Gran Snappy slid off the log into the water. "But why am I telling *you* this?" he asked. "If I was dying and I asked you to get me a pear from the Golden Pear Tree, you'd get to squabbling with the blue jays over a piece of bread. By the time you got back—and you probably wouldn't—I'd be dead and dried up and the turkey buzzards would be—"

"Oh, no, I'd bring you back a Golden Pear, Granddaddy, if the tree was still there," Mudslider cried. "I swear I would, if I could."

Gran Snappy said, "Humph!" Then he dangled in the

water and stared at Mudslider so hard that Mudslider wondered if the old turtle might be sizing him up for a snack anyway. "Say, how come you didn't die from the Pond Poisoning last summer when the other ones did?" Gran Snappy asked.

"I don't know, but I'm still here. I'm the same little old weak hungry thing now that I was last year," Mudslider said. "I'll never get as big as you."

"Well, be glad you're still alive and can get hungry. You eat the Old Gal's fruits and vegetables from now on instead of all the other stuff she throws out to us. There's been many a big dumb turtle dead today from eating stuff they didn't recognize. Now take that Ripper. Dumb as they come, but thinks he knows everything. I don't expect much out of him. At least you got good sense. Maybe I'll turn the Pond over to *you* someday." At that, Gran Snappy laughed. He closed his eyes, still laughing, and sank to the bottom of the Pond.

For the next few weeks, remembering Gran Snappy's advice, Mudslider only ate the Old Gal's apples, watermelons, and carrot tops, and there was plenty of that. Except for Gran Snappy, most of the other turtles didn't much seem to like them. They and Ripper preferred the white bread, the chicken necks, the pork chop bones, and the fish guts. To Mudslider's delight, he also found plenty of pears in the mud that had fallen from the Pond's pear tree.

But yet he wondered if the Great Golden Pear Tree was still by the Old Gal's nest. Did its pears really make Gran Snappy wise and strong? Could they make him strong, too?

One afternoon Mudslider had paused by the willow stump to speak to Gran Snappy. "Granddaddy," he called out, "don't I look bigger to you?"

Gran Snappy writhed suddenly in the water and moaned in reply. His eyes bulged. He pawed spastically at his big mouth with his front legs, gagged, and went limp.

Crooner the bullfrog watched from where he sat by a thatch of saw grass. Ripper, the other snappers, the pond slider and stinkpot turtles, the tadpoles, the skinks, the heron, the muskrat, and the rabbit watched, too. The cardinals, the grackles, and even the blue jays looked on silently in the trees.

"What's the matter, Granddaddy?" Mudslider asked, alarmed. "What's wrong with him?"

"Must be time for him to pass along the Pond to me," said Ripper. He snapped at Mudslider's right hind leg.

"Get gone," Mudslider snapped back, and hissed right in Ripper's face. "I gotta help Granddaddy!"

Mudslider paddled closer to Gran Snappy and peered up in his face. He couldn't lose the old turtle now. "Granddaddy, say something! Can't anybody do anything? What happened?"

"Greedy. Greedy. Greedy," Crooner finally said.

Mudslider turned back to Gran Snappy and saw a piece of something yellow dangling from his mouth. Mudslider took hold of the yellow object in his own small jaws. He pulled at it a little. Nothing happened. He jerked again. Gran Snappy gagged and jerked back. Mudslider hung on to the yellow piece, drifted to the bottom, and pulled back. He dug his little claws into the mud and pulled and jerked and tugged. Gran Snappy thrashed about in the water, choking.

Then an inch or so of the stuff slid from Gran Snappy's mouth. Seeing it, Mudslider jerked again. Foot firm to the ground, Mudslider told himself. Take your time, slow and steady, and jerk, pull, tug! Jerk, pull, tug! Suddenly Gran Snappy gave out a loud belch, and a big wad of the yellow material came hurtling out of his mouth. Mudslider rolled end over shell across the Pond bottom and finally came to a stop against a rock. He let loose of the yellow piece just before Ripper rushed over, gulped it down, and swam away.

Gran Snappy floated over to his log, where he sucked in air. Mudslider swam over to him, and together they bobbed, resting, by the log. Everyone applauded. "Grand-daddy, you okay?" Mudslider whispered. "C'mon, say you're gonna be all right."

Gran Snappy cleared his throat and nodded. "That thing got caught so deep in my craw I thought it was gonna strangle me to death. I thought that was a chicken skin, but it was a piece of plastic! I've been here choking for an hour and these fools have just lain around eye-balling me!"

"I'm glad you're okay. Boy, you should have seen how big your eyes got," Mudslider said. "You got cross-eyed a couple times, and then they bugged out, and slobber was—"

"All right, all right. Look here, I got to stop calling you Mudslider. That's no true hatch name for a snapping turtle, especially one who just saved my life, and I do thank you very much for it."

"I'm glad I was strong enough to do something, for once. Granddaddy, is Snappy your hatch name, too?"

Gran Snappy shook his head. "Snappy's my Pond name, my nickname. I'm Puller One. Say, I'm gonna call you Puller Two. Now you got a true hatching-out name. Turtles, this is Puller Two from now on."

"Puller Two?" Mudslider rolled the name around in his mouth. "Puller Two. Hey, that's all right. Puller Two. Yeah, that's me!"

"Maybe one of these days you'll even be the next ruler of the Pond," said Gran Snappy. He rolled his eyes over at Ripper. "At least *you* got common sense."

Mudslider paddled in circles around Gran Snappy, his little eyes glowing, snapping his beak, jerking his head.

"Slow down, Puller Two, you're making me dizzy. Now c'mon. Let me show you how to get around on land."

Recommended Readings on Proverbs and Sayings

Gleason, Norma, compiler and editor, *Proverbs from Around the World,* New York: Citadel Press, 1992.

Knappert, Jan, *The A–Z of African Proverbs,* London: Karnak House, 1989.

Leslan, Charlotte and Wolf, compilers, *African Proverbs,* White Plains, New York: Peter Pauper Press, 1985.

McKnight, Reginald, editor, *African American Wisdom,* the Classic Wisdom Collection, San Rafael, California: New World Library, 1994.

Quotes Plus; set of four titles using and discussing quotes from American, British, multicultural, and young adult literature, Logan, Iowa: Perfection Learning Corp., 1996.

Steele, Phillip W., *Ozark Tales and Superstitions,* Gretna, Louisiana: Pelican Publishing Company, 1990.

CPSIA information can be obtained at www.ICGtesting.com
Printed in the USA
LVOW07s2200100215

426543LV00001B/130/P